D0711435

A LESSER DAY

ANDREA SCRIMA

Spuyten Duyvil
New York City

Author's Acknowledgements:

My heartfelt gratitude goes to Christian von der Goltz and Barbara Jung, without whose continued encouragement and support this book would perhaps never have been written.

I'd also like to thank Nava Renek and Tod Thilleman of Spuyten Duyvil Press; Rebecca Morrison; Ingrid Wagner; the Senatsverwaltung für Wissenschaft, Forschung und Kultur in Berlin, Germany; and Erica Silverman and George Nicholson of Sterling Lord Literistic, New York.

Library of Congress Cataloging-in-Publication Data

Scrima, Andrea, 1960-
A lesser day / Andrea Scrima.

p. cm.

ISBN 978-1-933132-77-8
1. Memory–Fiction.
2. Brooklyn (New York, N.Y.)–Fiction.
3. Berlin (Germany)–Fiction.
4. Psychological fiction. I. Title.

PS3619.C75L47 2010
813'.6–dc22   2009050213

Printed in Canada.

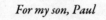

For my son, Paul

... see, now they vanish,
The faces and places, with the self which,
as it could, loved them,
To become renewed, transfigured,
in another pattern.

T.S. Eliot, *Little Gidding; Four Quartets*

EISENBAHNSTRASSE, and the moment I entered the studio for the first time again after returning from a two-week absence. Absurd that a quantity can exist, be verified, that a time can be measured, two weeks, anything can happen, nothing can happen in two weeks. A bundle of mail wedged under my arm, a travel bag in one hand and a sack of coal in the other. The sudden strangeness of the space, the strangeness of the plasterboard wall, so familiar and yet somehow too long, too high now. And how quickly this vision evaporated, returned to the usual, how quickly the wall became normal again. Cold, it was always so cold, and the little ceramic oven burnt out so quickly, the heat vanished from the room again so abruptly, but I didn't know that yet, I didn't know the winters there yet, I had only just finished the renovation when I had to drop everything and rush off to New York, now, now. It was November, the cold was just beginning to seep into the walls, freezing, I was always freezing, always pouring another bucket of coal into the oven, always emptying ashes, removing the tray as gingerly as I could to keep the fine red dust from flying up into my face, but I didn't know that yet, I had only just moved in when my mother called and told me to come. And that night spent waiting in the dark, waiting for it to be time to leave for the airport, for the alarm clock to drill its incessant beep into the walls of my stomach, my bag packed and waiting, the walls waiting, the blood in my veins waiting. How strange the space looked, strange to think of it being empty these past two weeks, two weeks in which perhaps a little dust settled on the table, on the desk, in which a few calls were recorded on the answering machine, a few hang-ups, two weeks in which nearly nothing happened, in which the lamp remained where it was, the table where it was, the cup where it was, the tea I'd drunk the night before, there, where I left it, inconceivable. Yet now, after two weeks' absence, I open the door and it's not the same, something has changed, something feels evil, I've brought a stowaway back with me, a demon that kept itself hidden throughout the journey, which now leapt out invisibly, vanished into the walls noiselessly, infusing the space with a fear that never went away again, a fear of a deeper, blacker dark, and I was allowed to keep the bedroom door ajar, a crack, and I crept out of bed and along the creaking floorboards to peer down the long hallway to the narrow strip of living room visible beyond, listening intently to the muffled sounds of the television, soothing me, the muffled sounds of safety. And you were still alive, your stacks of quarters for the bridge toll carefully lined along the edge of the piano each night, your lunch in a brown paper bag in the refrigerator and always something drawn in ballpoint pen on the inside of the napkin, the lunch I made for you each night, each night.

EISENBAHNSTRASSE. The window set into the wall separating the living space from the studio, and the paintings drying in the tall racks behind it. How I sat at the kitchen table in the morning, drinking a cup of coffee and wondering whether to heat the studio that day, whether it was worth the price of the coal. How I sat, drinking and looking through the window at the canvases leaning against the wooden beams, barely grazing the ceiling, and through them at the painting hanging on the side wall, the painting hanging on the back wall, and always a slight tinge of red spread across it, reflected from the façade of an electronics factory. The paintings I worked on for three years, over and over and not knowing why, not knowing where they would take me or what I was trying to find, and the paint building up layer by layer, inch by inch, six paintings, five by ten feet in size; three years. I used to calculate how much longer it would take for the walls to close in, layer by layer, one painting on the back wall, one painting on the

4

side wall with the oven pipe running above it to the far corner of the room, trying to hold the heat a little longer before it escaped up the chimney, maybe it kept the space a little warmer, I don't know, and the paint building up layer by layer, a quarter of an inch a month, three inches a year, times three, times six. And then, how I finally painted them over, covered them in an opaque layer of white, and then another, so as not to have to see them anymore, see my failure, another layer of white, and then another. And how some of the pigments bled slowly through from underneath as the paint began to dry.

EISENBAHNSTRASSE, and the window above the desk. I used to unlatch the hook and poke my head out to check up on the cat; I used to call his name, and he'd come running along the top of the brick wall behind the garbage bins, look up and stop, his mouth opening in a little cat cry inaudible at that distance. Sometimes, though, he was sleeping on one of the car seats that filled the crowded shed of the car mechanic, who always kept a little food ready in a dish and who sat outside on a folding chair in the courtyard with his wife and daughter in the evening. And I was always afraid of the landlady's nine-year-old son, afraid he'd do something to the cat, but what, he was only a little boy, yet it was a feeling I had, a feeling that never let go of me, strange. He used to wander around the courtyard, poking at things with a stick, looking up at my window now and again as though he'd guessed my thoughts, as though he were afraid of being caught, but perhaps he was only perceiving my suspicion, made uneasy by it, nothing more. And then the cat got locked in the mechanic's shed one weekend, and I didn't know where he lived, or what his telephone number was, Ivo was his name, a Croatian émigré. I called to the cat, and he answered, crying, and I waited for Ivo to come and unlock the shed so I could carry him home. The day passed, the cat crying, scratching at the walls and crying, and then I finally found a spot where one of the wooden slats was rotten, and I knocked it through, thinking the cat could escape, but no, I had only broken into the back of a locked cupboard. How long it took to finally find another weakened spot where I could pry a board back somewhat, just enough to let a cat slip through, and how he rubbed up against me in the end, circling in and out between my legs as we went upstairs, running up a few steps ahead and waiting at the top of each flight for me to stroke his thick black fur, our little ritual, his back arching and his tail shooting up in pleasure. I opened the door to the studio and fed the cat and waited for Ivo to come, and the next day, and the day after that, to apologize for breaking into his shed, to offer to fix it, and then a week went by without Ivo, and then another week, and he never came back, never again, because the war had begun, and it gradually dawned on me that Ivo had gone home to do his patriotic duty, and the car wrecks continued to rust in the courtyard, and the wife, the daughter never returned. I moved out of Eisenbahnstrasse a year and a half later, the war having only just begun, and who knows when the rent stopped coming in, when the landlady became alarmed, when her son began standing on his tip-toes to peer into Ivo's shed, when he began throwing rocks at the windowpanes.

HOW MANY TIMES has my thinking become caught in a loop; how many times has my mind circled around a certain word, an expression that passed over a face and vanished, around and around, trying to get closer, but to what. That feeling of something being there, circling around and around; but what. That uneasy feeling of something about to be revealed, the quiet panic. And then, the moment of realization, its anaesthetizing effect. I see this, understand this, yet I don't see, I don't understand. The amnesia that follows, when the mind carefully buries its new discovery, only digging it up some time later when it's certain of being alone, unobserved, turning it over and over, sniffing at it as though it were a dried-out bone.

FIDICINSTRASSE; the sight of the apartment again after all this time. The jungle of green in the garden out back, the swarms of chirping birds in the plum trees planted ten, fifteen years ago by a Turkish immigrant who couldn't stand the damp and the cold seeping up from the floor and moved to a second-story flat at the front of the building instead. A great commotion of sparrows hopping from branch to branch, from time to time flying away in rash departure; the sound of hundreds of tiny wings flapping. The hedge Frau Chran planted thirty, forty years ago and the ongoing difference in opinion about how it should be trimmed, Frau Chran always wanting to be able to see over it, you and I always wanting our privacy from the people passing by on the sidewalk behind. How it got shorter from year to year as Frau Chran grew older and shrank. And then she was bedridden, and the hedge grew high and wild, buried under a tangle of wild hops that left welts on my arms every time I pulled the tough, hairy vines out of the branches and down from the trees to let in a little more light. And now, my huge black suitcases standing in the hall, packed to the brim, packed to the maximum weight allowance each time, no, a few pounds above, always a few pounds above. My entire life in those suitcases, compact, portable; my relief each time the wheels didn't break off. The long flight behind me, the wait in Brussels: the ubiquitous Belgian tapestry work, Belgian chocolate. Then, the shorter flight to Berlin Tempelhof and the anxious moment when I saw your face on the other side of the control barrier. Not knowing how it was going to be between us now, after all this time.

FIDICINSTRASSE, and Bettembourg shuffling up and down the block with his Dalmatian limping slowly next to him, up and down, up and down, gazing expressionlessly at anyone approaching as though it were a bit blind. Its limping gait, its dry, matte fur drained of any shine it once possessed; its head cocked to one side and that look of confusion. And the moment someone passed, it would break into an insane, vicious bark, taking anyone who didn't already know this by surprise, because even those most cautious with dogs, even the most wary weren't prepared for the slowness of the dog's reaction, the dim-witted gaze changing into vicious fury, the delay. And Bettembourg, with his rosy cheeks, his baby skin, held onto the leash and smiled idiotically, and some of the tenants couldn't take it anymore, couldn't take the smell of urine, couldn't take the idiotic smile, this dog driven mad by a madman, and changed to the other side of the street. A petition went around when the woman who lived beneath him moved out because Bettembourg had been relieving himself in the corner for so long that urine finally began seeping through the ceiling. And when I found myself suddenly sitting opposite him in the S-Bahn* at Alexanderplatz, he didn't recognize me, although we must have passed each other at least once a day for the past seven or eight years. How I hurried by him late one night, full of disgust at the sight of him standing in the dark in the building's entrance with his pants pulled down, smeared with excrement, crying, and the dog barking insanely, incessantly; how I only learned a short time later, after he died, that he must have been very sick, he must have been in terrible pain that night, he was already dying, sixty-two years old, or sixty-three, with his rosy cheeks, his baby skin.

* elevated train

FIDICINSTRASSE, and how easy it would have been to break in; how the door used to slam shut from the wind sometimes as I stood in the hallway talking to Frau Chran, and how I used to walk through her dark apartment and climb out of her window over the little footstool she kept underneath it and then back into our own window from the garden. Sometimes I went next door to loosen the long straps alongside the window frames and let down the heavy shutters for her, lingering for a moment over the pictures on the wall: a son fallen somewhere in Russia; a husband in an ill-fitting suit made of coarse fabric. Knickknacks and the smell of damp and coal dust and mold mixing together and rising up from the motley carpet remnants covering the floor to keep out the cold. All the little devices Frau Chran had inserted between the lowermost branches of the hedge over the years to ward off dogs and prowlers; lengths of chicken wire and metal racks from discarded refrigerators tied together with bits of twisted wire. And the rubbish from the street caught in between: old schnapps bottles, empty cigarette packages, scraps of paper erased by the rain. How I used to get on my hands and knees and gather the garbage out from under the hedge, dragging a large plastic bag behind me, my arms and face becoming scratched from the thorns of the wild bushes growing in between. And then, the next day, the first beer bottle tossed over the hedge, the first discarded newspaper trapped among the branches. How we woke up one morning to find it cut back to a third of its girth, cut so deeply into the branches that half of them died off and never recovered, but that came later. We ran out back and stared at the long pile of severed branches left there on the sidewalk as though some horrendous crime had taken place, and then we found out who the culprit was, the red-faced pensioner from next door who walked his dog every evening out back behind the garden and who was always stopping and peering into our bedroom window with a sidelong glance, calling Ina, Iiiiiii-*na!* as the dog crawled through the hedge to do its business beneath the rose bushes. How he must have crept out early that Sunday morning and cut the hedge with hand clippers to avoid waking us up, an old man, it's amazing he didn't have a heart attack right there, or a stroke, with his beet-red face, his high blood pressure. Cut along an imaginary line he held to be where the sidewalk, where public property officially began, *öffentliches Strassenland!,* * as he screamed in indignation, shaking a trembling fist after we'd climbed the three flights of stairs and knocked on his door. How I used to dream of hiring a crane and clipping the geraniums on his balcony right down to the roots, boiling with rage as I looked out onto the shaky remainder of our hedge and the knee-deep pile of severed branches.

* public property

THIS DISTURBANCE in the fabric of things; how can I describe it?—A difficulty with the present tense. I feel this moment, taste it, yet it eludes me; it's as though I were merely remembering it, dreaming it. Now, I think, now—yet nothing I tell myself can break the spell.

FIDICINSTRASSE, when the piano was still in the little room, my studio in the big room with the ceramic coal oven in one corner and the canvases stacked up against the wall, far too large to maneuver easily now. The way the tiles reflected the light from the windows, little specks of green from the trees outside rippling across the shiny yellow surface. How the air used to weigh down in the chimney on certain days and seep through all the tiny cracks between the tiles, filling the apartment with the acrid smell of soot; how I stretched a number of smaller canvases and worked on them at the table by the window, listening to the radio with the late afternoon winter darkness outside. The way the cold fluorescent glow from the studio illuminated the hedge in the garden, and how shallow the light was, how black the branches behind. Frau Chran used to talk about when the street out back was just a dirt path, with none of the traffic there is today, none of the lines of cars in the early morning headed for the police station, the department of motor vehicles. Nothing but fields all the way to the airport, even after the banners with swastikas had long since been removed from the façades and the Americans began flying provisions into the city. And now, the post-war advertising murals peeling off the cemetery walls in thick, fragile curls of cement; the booths of automobile insurance companies lining the street beyond. Groups of squealing children passing by the hedge every morning, coming from the kindergarten down the block, and later in the day, actors from the alternative theater, once in a while singing a show tune with a verve, a zest that rose above the drone of the radio and briefly filled the room with the make-up, the costumes, the bright lights of the cabaret. And the news always came on at the hour, and I used to put down the brush and turn up the volume. How it was nearly always Sarajevo, every day Sarajevo and snipers. A brief reprieve; a group of children playing outside for the first time in months, their exhilarated breath steaming in the cold, dry air, their cheeks flushed crimson. How I sat and listened, sat and stared out the window as an image of blood seeping into snow appeared before my eyes, spreading slowly, like the thick sugary syrup seeping into the balls of crushed ice the Puerto Rican vendor sells from his little wagon on the corner of Marcy Avenue, scraping it off a large block and dropping the ball into a paper cone. And Frau Chran used to talk about how the corpses were piled up on Marheinekeplatz towards the end of the war, where large umbrellas protect the restaurant tables from the sun and chestnut trees cast their wide shadows over the playground, big broad areas of shade dotted with little specks of bright light.

FIDICINSTRASSE, and the summer all the children of the building gathered in the courtyard outside our windows to play. Martin used to rile them up, chasing after them and making them scream in fear and delight, Martin, who'd sat alone with a malevolent look in the corner of the courtyard the year we moved in, wordlessly eyeing everyone who walked by and digging lines into the dust with a stick. And then he changed suddenly, or so it seemed, assuming a protective authority over the other children of the building, picking the littlest ones up and twirling them around until they squealed, and then gently lowering them back down onto their feet again. That was the summer the children began growing wilder, yelling and running around in circles and bouncing a soccer ball against the wall of the building, and always within inches of a windowpane, inches, and how a windowpane finally broke, and then another, and all of the children suddenly vanished. And then I asked Martin in some time later under some sort of pretext and with an eye to the new panes of glass we had just set in, the fresh putty, hoping to make friends. How polite he was; how quickly I became addicted to his smile. And Ulrich, who used to come home stumbling and singing from the Fidicinclause at seven o'clock in the morning with Martin's mother Inge, who could never quite make heads or tails of Martin, came down one day and pulled him across the yard by the ear in front of the other children, Ulrich, who used to stop by when we were renovating the apartment to watch, to give us advice, and then he'd linger in the doorway, the smell of alcohol on his breath slowly drifting into the room, and we were always trying to guess what he wanted from us, perhaps it was just the feeling of being taken seriously, nothing more. And poor Ulrich died in the hospital within a week of his old buddy Hotte, whom he wouldn't speak to for years after a drunken brawl in the Fidicinclause one night, whom he passed every day in the courtyard without a word, straightening up out of his usual slouch and looking the other way with an offended frown, but that came later. How Martin's face darkened every time Ulrich was nearby, who was so cruel and helpless with this wild boy. And then I found a severed cat's tail one day in the garden out back, and then a cat's paw, and I immediately had to think of Martin throwing it over the hedge, Martin dropping it from the balcony three flights above. How I stared at these furry things, how it took some time for this image to impress itself upon me; how I stared at them lying in the grass for the longest time, feeling that I must be mistaken and turning them over gingerly with a twig to take a closer look.

FIDICINSTRASSE, and the ivy I planted out back. It had just begun to take when the notice went up that the façade was going to be painted. And so we dug it up again and carried it into the apartment, and all of its leaves fell off as we watched the workers trample through the roses to put up the scaffolding. And then, several months later, when the last of the metal poles and boards were finally carried away, the sight of the devastated garden and the plum trees standing there, two short stumps sticking out of the dirt and drips of paint all over the ground; how it took another two years before the ivy began growing again, as though it preferred to wait and see before giving it another try.

How can I begin to sort out the days, the weeks; everything was different, wasn't it? Walking through a turnstile at Delancey Street, suddenly seized with a need to speak to you; now. And what were you doing that very moment, and how far was I from your thoughts. How to go back and revise my conception of the past: what was happening then, or then— a useless endeavor.

BEDFORD AVENUE. The layers of dust everywhere, the piles of useless junk, the foreign sounds. I cleared a table and unlocked one of the suitcases and began arranging some of the things into careful stacks; the odd feeling of undoing this tightly packed, economic arrangement, this transitory suitcase order which seemed more plausible, more real than the new order I was attempting to create. The books I'd read over the past few months in transit, lined up now on my makeshift desk; the paper models of the installations tacked to the wall, and next to them a subway map with its brightly colored lines running in tight bundles all over the schematic contours of the boroughs. And my eyes tracing them from station to station in imagined excursion, locked away inside this dusty, cluttered loft without any windows on the top floor of a former two-story garage, with only a homemade skylight to let in a little air. I had to run up to the roof and climb over a fire wall to drag the heavy Plexiglas cover back over the opening any time it rained, but the air stayed heavy and hot and I eventually left the skylight open and mopped up the puddles of rainwater instead, but that came later. And the paintbrushes, the camera and tripod, arranged to the side and already with the remote air of things that would never be used here, never be touched, a helpless attempt at setting up camp once again. The next day, sitting at the table under the skylight reading the newspaper in the inconceivable heat, the sweat dripping from my temples and forming dark dots that spread on the printed page before me like tiny explosions. My eyes, drawn again and again to the marks on the wall left behind by countless sheets of paper, brush-strokes fanning out from crisp-edged, empty frames, and everywhere drips, smears, smudges, and I, staring at them again and again, unable to concentrate on anything else, jumped up from my chair and took down the subway map and all the paper models, intent upon giving the wall a quick layer of paint. I bought two gallons of white interior from the Polish hardware store down the street, and afterwards, when I tacked the paper models to the wall again, it looked much cleaner, yet it changed nothing, really, it was as apparent as it had been before that I would wait here the next few weeks for you to come, nothing more, wait here with my little desk ensemble and the freshly painted walls and the stacks of someone else's things cleared away to one end of the loft and the newspapers piling up day by day, cutting out a picture now and again and pinning it to the wall, the only evidence of my presence.

BEDFORD AVENUE, and the two cats that had to be fed as part of the summer sublet. The heavy smell of the cat litter box in the sweltering heat, unpleasant enough, and then the balls of cat hair everywhere, collecting in every corner and covering the couch, the chairs, although I brushed them every evening, gleaning whole bushels of fine hair out of their thick, inexhaustible furs. And some of it always flying around, into the nose, the mouth; unavoidable. The one cat loved it, loved to be brushed, arching her back and snorting in pleasure; the other cat didn't, but submitted to the procedure obediently. How this cat kept his distance, coming for his dinner in the evening and then crying at the door to be let out again immediately afterwards. I never knew where he went until I found him on the roof one night, where I spread out a blanket to cool off from the oppressive heat of the loft, although the air stood just as still as it did inside and the tar was still baking from the afternoon sun. How he kept a discreet distance here, as well, although he always remained within view, on a fire wall, a chimney, his yellow eyes glowing and his black fur invisible in the darkness. And then I discovered him one afternoon with a dirty sock from someone's laundry basket; how he ran across the loft with the sock in his mouth and suddenly stopped, glanced around before letting it drop to the floor, and uttered a mournful cry. And then, how he seemed to wake up from a trance; how he gave the sock a quick look, shook a paw, and hurried away.

BEDFORD AVENUE. Sitting at the table with a pair of scissors in my hand, about to cut a picture out of the international news section of the *New York Times*. A hill, a horizon curving across the middle of the image; three or four men photographed from below with a thick rope slung taut over their shoulders, hoisting a coffin out of its grave. And the photograph's caption, how little it told, relatives unearthing an uncle, a brother in preparation for the flight from Bosnia, unwilling to leave even their dead behind. And I, wondering how they could take all they would need, provisions and water and clothing, what else do refugees take with them when there's too little time to prepare for the unknown perils of an uncertain journey. And the coffins, with no idea of when or where they would be able to bury them again, where do they put the coffins, on the roofs of their cars? What do they do when they're forced to leave their vehicles behind, do they carry them on their shoulders, four to a coffin, coffin upon coffin

in an endless procession of the dead, the soon
to be killed?

I TURN MY ATTENTION to this moment, try to comprehend its immediacy, to trust in its reality; I tell myself that this is the present, this moment and no other. I gaze around and see the faint imprint of dried raindrops on the window glass, see my hands resting on the table before me. My mind runs after this moment, and the next one, and the one after that; I instruct myself to commit every detail to memory, but I cannot, and I cannot exist in the present, knowing that I am bound to forget the greater part of what I see around me.

EISENBAHNSTRASSE. The weeks after you died, and then the months that followed, as though measured in some other, more malleable, unit of time. How elastic everything seemed, as though things could slip into another form at any moment, as though the very space surrounding me could loop in on itself, become turned inside out without warning. Sometimes I imagined that I was already an old woman merely dreaming of being young, and sometimes I imagined that I was already dead, or a mother who had just lost a son and not the other way around, as though your death had induced time to tunnel back inside me somehow. How I floated through the days that followed with my eyes wide open and my voice sounding as though it were coming from somewhere outside my own skull. And the jobs at the theater that winter, stapling the long canvas banners to the floor and rolling the paint over them while the set designers and production assistants came and went around me; how I placed a large fan at one end of the banner and went down to the cafeteria to wait for it to dry, hiding away in a corner with a cup of coffee and a book. And on some nights, in between dress rehearsals, the actors would begin drifting in with their make-up and costumes, thronging around the cash register and the refrigerated glass vitrines. What, one of them cried out—no fruit salad? *No more muffins?* Exaggerated expressions; boisterous laughter. How I watched them drift in and gradually fill the cafeteria, and then closed the book and laid it on the table before me as a man in a powdered wig and a plumed hat picked up an empty parfait glass from the rack of used trays and called out in a woeful tone, *this might have been your fruit salad, my lad.* And then a woman with her bosom neatly tucked into the bodice of a dirndl bent over my table with a conspiratorial wink to ask me if the other chairs were free, snatched up my book, and held it out at arm's length, enunciating the title as though it were a papal edict and gesturing solemnly as

I shrank back into my corner with an overwhelming urge to cry. Where are you; where are you. I hurried back upstairs, hung up my gas mask by its rubber strap, fetched my coat from the locker, and made for the door without a word. And then, remembering the impending rent, I thought the better of it and carried my coat back to the locker, washed out the brushes that were already beginning to stiffen, stretched a string for a base line, and began sketching out the letters spelling the title of the next premiere. How I painted them in, kneeling on the hard wooden floor and tracing the curves with a trembling hand, thinking about how much I hated the theater, hated everything about it, hated everything dramatic, everything theatrical. Those were the months I used to write myself little notes: watch out when you're crossing the street; watch out when you're handling the drill. An absent-mindedness I was unable to shake, and that feeling of being under water, or under glass. How cold and damp it was, how

I froze in my thin jacket as we walked around the botanical garden in Paris that November, and then, suddenly, we found ourselves in the tropical climate section, and then in the desert climate section, and how I wanted to stay in the desert, never leave this desert with its cactus and its rare, lavish flowers, protected and warm forever. You, and you. A day or two later we went up the Eiffel Tower, diligent tourists, and you told me that you wanted to be cremated; you were leaving your ashes to a friend to be used as a pigment, you said. What a dismal color it will make, I answered; ash grey, mixed with linseed oil on a glass palette, *I wouldn't want to paint with that.* And then you photographed me with an antenna in the background, motioning for me to move a little more to the left so that the antenna would appear to be sprouting out of the top of my head, but that came later, I only discovered that later, after I'd picked up the developed pictures. And what do I have from that week, still: a red plastic folder; a white cotton bedspread stolen from the hotel and later dyed a deep shade of rose, which I hung in front of our bedroom window and which gradually faded to a pale pink over the years; the photos I took of myself in an automatic booth somewhere near the Gare du Nord, killing time until my train left for Berlin, haunted by the nagging sense that I would never be seeing you again— these four photographs with a blue background and that look of being under water, or under glass, two in a drawer somewhere and the other two completely forgotten until I caught a brief glimpse of them years later, when the official at the Ausländerpolizei* opened my file and briskly leafed through the pages as I sat across the desk under the harsh glare of the fluorescent light, filling out an application for a right of permanent residence. And how odd it was to see them unexpectedly among all these formulas I'd filled out and signed over the years, with two neat holes punched into the left margin and filed away in a manila folder; how it felt as though

I had stumbled into a trap, confronted with some kind of awful and irrefutable evidence.

* immigration authorities

EISENBAHNSTRASSE, and how we worked together on a theater production, was that ten years ago? Eleven? And then another, and the carpenter named Freddy who nearly never said a word: his tabloid newspapers, his wurst sandwiches wrapped in plastic foil in the refrigerator with the wood-grain contact paper curling up at the corners; how he spent the day cutting wood and putting together the raw constructions for the sets, having never gone to see a single production, having never been interested, having never been invited, perhaps, with a pair of tickets to the premiere tucked inside a clean white envelope with his first and last name printed carefully on the outside, but nobody knew Freddy's last name, Freddy was always just Freddy. How we had to work through the night making changes for a set designer who was very, very friendly, and very, very worried, difficulties with the director, difficulties with the set, and how I broke out in hives at the sight of him smiling in between the buckets of paint, needless buckets from colors not quite hit upon, always a little off, a little more red, a little more ochre, and then it was all too dark, masses of paint, and all of it far too dark, and how many more gallons of white were needed to lighten it up enough, what in the world are we going to do with all this superfluous paint, all these useless buckets. And all of this occurring backstage with a production going on around us and stagehands carrying things to and fro. Then, the sound of the orchestra and the shadow of an actress ascending a stair under a spotlight, projected onto the curtain behind her and visible on the reverse side, where we paused, brush in hand, and watched her silhouette in astonishment: the raised head, the outstretched arms, a grand finale; crescendo and applause. The few things we still have from there: a discarded vacuum cleaner; an old mattress; two huge stretchers Freddy once made; a small desk which was far too beautiful to be a prop and which I talked you into stealing; a roll of sandpaper for the sanding machine, half of

it gone, half of it left, even now, after ten years,
or eleven.

EISENBAHNSTRASSE, and the job we never got paid for, painting circus wagons for a Buffalo Bill show pieced together with the straggly remnants of the former East German state circus gone bankrupt. The animals out in Hoppegarten, waiting in their cages with nothing to do, watching, alert. Baboons throwing nuts and anything else they could grab out of a belligerence I didn't think existed outside the human species; scrambling up to the bars of the cage and kicking against them in defiance. And the camels; a polar bear; two elephants swinging their trunks in unison; a panther crouched in a dark corner, silent and invisible except for his glowing yellow eyes. And a lion, pacing back and forth with the restlessness of an intelligent animal accustomed to activity. How the lion picked up on my movement and followed me when I walked by the cage, and when I stopped and turned, how he did the same, as supremely alert as a cat following a toy with its gaze. We longed to believe that we could let him out of the cage to play, that we could stroke his beautiful fur and he'd arch his back and groan in pleasure, that he wouldn't maul us to shreds. The animal attendant and the buckets of raw meat he threw into the animals' cages; how he peered at us with a taciturn and sour gaze. I went off to watch the elephants swinging their trunks in wide arcs, back and forth, back and forth, standing side by side with their huge bodies touching gently; were they passing the time, or were they trying to dispel their anxiety, I could never tell. We eventually learned that soon there wouldn't be any money left to feed the animals, that they would have to be sold off individually wherever they could; that it would be nearly impossible to find a buyer for two elephants—and how little their chances of survival would be in the event of separation.

THAT ONE MOMENT, that one detail which has remained in my memory, but why, it was nothing of importance, nothing occurred, a shaft of light falling obliquely across a sidewalk, a rustling of leaves. And all of it burned into my mind with a brilliance and a clarity, every detail branded upon my inner eye like the crisp letters of a printed word I do not understand. I say light, leaves, yet none of it can convey the mythical significance it holds for me. And does some larger thing lie concealed within it, and why have I forgotten it—forgotten the sudden realization of self-betrayal for instance, there, then, with this sidewalk, these leaves—or is it a random product, jettison caught up in the craggy recesses of a mind.

BEDFORD AVENUE; standing in front of the subway map, pronouncing the names and tasting the residue they left behind on my tongue. How far removed they seemed, as though from another world, another time; how unlikely it seemed that I could go outside with this map in my pocket and actually board a train. And then I finally overcame my lethargy and walked down Bedford Avenue and descended the steps to the subway as the sweat trickled down between my breasts; how I got on an air-conditioned train with no clear plan in mind, reached up for the overhead bar, and watched the goose-bumps appear on my bare arm as the sweat on my skin grew cold. I changed trains several times, first at Union Square, then at Grand Central, combing the crowd as the subway pulled into each station, my eyes darting from one face to another, searching for someone I might know, anyone at all, inconceivable to have grown up in a city and recognize no one, absolutely no one. My eyes shifted from the subway window and the river of people rushing past outside up to the row of advertisements above them, hotlines for wife abuse, child abuse, centers for cosmetic surgery, dental surgery, with a picture of Doctor So-and-So and his signature underneath, topped off with a medical sort of flourish. And then, suddenly, I found myself on the way up to the Bronx and decided to get off at 149th Street to see if the old building was still there, when was the last time I went, I must have been a child. I walked down Brook Avenue without recognizing a single building, a single tree, turned the corner at 148th Street, and walked towards St. Ann's, counting out the even numbers on the south side of the street as they approached 516, the building my great-grandparents purchased after they arrived in the country, the building my mother grew up in, my grandmother grew up in, two long rows of five-story buildings on either side of the street with railroad flats two to a floor and women in long skirts and aprons sweeping the sidewalk every evening. Here was 514, a two-story building set back somewhat from the others; there was a child's tricycle lying on its side on a small concrete patio out front with weeds sprouting up between the cracks. I walked on to the next building and saw the numerals 518 nailed into the wood above the door, and then I stopped and retraced my steps; I must have passed it by, I thought, but there was no 516, only a building with the number 514, and another with the number 518, both of comparatively recent construction, but no 516, and I stood there, gazing at number 514, then at number 518, and realized that the building must have been torn down long ago, after the neighborhood had turned into a slum. And later, after the lots were redrawn and new buildings erected during a phase of urban renewal, 516 simply vanished from the row of addresses on East 148th Street altogether, and I stood here, where the front door to the building must have been, picturing my mother sitting on the front steps as a child, my grandmother, a child, here, on this very spot where the building once stood, manifested now in nothing more than a gap in a numerical sequence. I stood there for some time studying the buildings and the sizes of the lots, unable to explain how an address could have vanished, the newer buildings being no larger, no wider than the older ones had been, they wouldn't have taken up the extra space to make an entire lot vanish like that, I thought, and I walked down the street and turned the corner my mother had turned every day throughout her childhood on her way to the grammar school, across the street from the park, where the tough boys used to slide down the big granite rocks on cardboard boxes and tall trees grew out of the crevices in between, littered now with old newspapers and crushed beer cans and small piles of used syringes scattered among the underbrush.

Bedford Avenue: taking the train to the ferry and traveling out to Staten Island to see my mother; borrowing the car to drive up to the cemetery. How it took some time before I found the grave, searching among the rows of small headstones decorated with bouquets of wilted flowers and American flags washed pale by the rain. And how hard it was to find anything in the new section, where the cemetery borders on Todt Hill Road; how everything looked alike, acres of mown lawn on treeless hills and rows upon rows of uniform plots, like a model, a miniature suburbia, until the sight of your name engraved in stone sent a sharp stab to my heart, as though I were seeing it for the first time. Once, on your birthday, I found myself passing another cemetery and went in to wander around in the snow, thinking that you'd have turned eighty today, but that came later. I stopped in front of a gravestone that read *Nach fleißiger Arbeit und erfüllter Pflicht** and suddenly had to think of your little shoeshine corner in the basement with the metal shoe form screwed into a stud in the wall and the wooden brushes lined up in a neat row. Sometimes I made the trip out to Staten Island to escape the heat of the loft, climbing down the basement stairs and thinking about how huge it once seemed, when we used to skate back and forth on our metal roller skates, when we used to jump around on the pogo stick, digging little round pockmarks into the cement floor after the rubber tip got lost somewhere. And then I decided to give the walls a coat of paint, and I cleared the stacks of furniture away and moved all the old paintings to one wall and took down the screens from the windows, brushing the dried leaves and spider webs off the oxidized aluminum and scrubbing them clean under the garden hose out back. How I taped sheets of the Staten Island Advance to the floor and dipped the roller into the tray of paint with my mother looking on, and how she pointed out that this had all been my idea. And why was I doing this again, why was I always painting everything white? The little ceramic tiles glued to the inside of the window well: how nobody ever got around to grouting them, the white ones where Barbara's room used to be, the little square brown ones where my room used to be, Lisa's room used to be, back when the basement was sectioned off with imitation wood paneling and stucco ceilings, when the three of us moved downstairs to make room for Grandma, but Grandma died before she had to watch the first tenants take her place upstairs. The mirror that used to be in Barbara's room, with the frame painted bright red, everything in Barbara's room being white or red, or white and red; how the mirror is hanging in Laura's bathroom on Ninth Street to this day. And the sewer that used to back up into my room every time it rained, seeping under a low door on hinges cut into the wall; how I glued a thin sheet of cork to it and pinned my drawings up, penciled heads of John Lennon and Jimi Hendrix copied from record album covers with the faces carefully shaded and the highlights picked out with an eraser. Again and again, I wandered around the basement that summer, into the tool room, where rows of jars containing screws and bolts hung from the low ceiling, or into the recreation room with the indoor/outdoor rug and all of the things my brother left behind, computers, electronic components, a dismantled piano, crates and crates of papers, as though he hadn't long since gotten married and bought a house and started a family of his own. And all the old paintings stacked in the corner, the dresser, the trunk, my little stash of possessions, as though a part of me had never moved out, as though this were my little place to crawl back to, just in case, and I thought about the two of us, my brother and I, each of us with a piece of territory staked out, each of us with a place to return to, even now, in this vast empire of our childhood.

* after [a life of] diligent work and fulfilled duty

BEDFORD AVENUE, and the night before you came to New York. How I had been waiting; sweating through the hot days and walking the baking asphalt streets and waiting; and now, how I sat listening to your voice on the telephone with my eyes shut tight, suspended in the space it created around me. And you were in that state of anxiety prior to departure; you were coming tomorrow, and you hadn't begun to pack yet, dead tired and a flight at six in the morning. And I would be meeting you at the airport tomorrow afternoon, I would see you emerge through the gates with a crumpled newspaper under your arm and a look of groggy confusion and be seized with the impulse to turn around before your searching eyes could locate me in the crowd of excited onlookers, and run away.

A DAY, AN HOUR without contradiction. To have a feeling, to have it once and to retain it without ambivalence, without another flip of the coin. How many days spent immobile, waiting for these twirling bits of thought to slowly settle down at the bottom of the jar, afraid to move, afraid to stir up the commotion again, and every thought containing its antipode, every insight bearing the imprint of its opposite, and all the while struggling to locate one premise that can serve as a fundament to build upon, as an axis to revolve around, one feeling, one basic truth not destined for revision, for refutation. Not to spend another afternoon groping around in the dark—where did it go, where did it go— another afternoon, another day.

EISENBAHNSTRASSE; the futon spread out on the floor of the studio, and my brother stretched across it with his long feet hanging over the edge, sleeping off the jet lag. His travel case in the corner near the coal oven, open and sprawling with jeans and shirts and underwear, and beside it a pair of sweaty socks and a plastic bag of duty-free chocolate. I gazed at his sleeping body and thought about how well I knew it, and how I'd known it through every stage of growth, known it when his shoulder blades were tiny and fragile and we used to take baths together in the yellow-tiled tub, staring into the bubbles and imagining ourselves inside them; floating the shampoo bottle, the bar of soap like little boats across a lake. I suddenly had to think of him taking apart the radio when he was still too small to speak, scattering the parts all over the living room rug; how I had to gather them all up again after he was tucked into bed. And my little brother, playing the villain now, towering above me in a threatening pose, casting a long, black,

jagged shadow and laughing the sinister laugh
we used to imitate from the Saturday morning
cartoons. Our private joke; his revenge for
all the years I pushed him around, dunked him
in the pool. What a terrible sister I was, taking
advantage of the difference in age, the difference
in size, and all the tall tales I told him: how he
believed every word. We spent all our free time
together, glued to each other's side, entire sum-
mers under water in the pool out back, the skin
on our feet shriveling, our fingertips shriveling,
jumping up and down wildly in the water and
making waves, higher and higher, pulling ourselves up onto the edge of the pool and throwing
ourselves back in, laughing and shrieking and
jumping wildly and pretending we were at high
sea, shipwrecked, exhilarated, the water splashing over the edge of the pool and flooding the
ground around below. And then, exhausted,
we'd cling to the side of the pool, breathing in
the smell of the blue plastic lining in the sun and
bouncing up and down with the waves until the

water grew calm again, and then we'd take turns counting the seconds: who can stay under water longer, who can swim more lengths without coming up for air, trying to break the record each time until our lips turned blue and our eyes were red and bleary from the chlorine. I was always the one who made up the rules, and sometimes, imperiously, I changed them on a sudden whim. And now, my brother lying there on the futon, fast asleep; the first time we saw each other after the funeral, his first time abroad. How he took apart my broken vacuum cleaner and fixed the motor and put it back together again, how he fixed my bicycle, but that came later. How I had to go back and forth to the store several times a day to carry all the groceries; his disappointment that you couldn't buy exactly the same things as you could in Waldbaum's, a gallon of Florida orange juice, Thomas' English Muffins. And I was always pushing him to try something new, Königsberger Klopse for instance; we stood in front of Max and Moritz arguing, I explaining that it was similar to a hamburger, only better, and he finally giving in with a dark, silent fury. How he liked it in the end and forgot all about his resistance, his stubborn refusal, but that came later. And now we were like two orphans who'd forgotten to leave a trail of breadcrumbs behind, lost in a dark wood and afraid, and I thought: I'll never leave you, I'll protect you, but I knew it wasn't true, I knew that he'd be gone again in a few weeks, and that our magic bond was a thing of long ago, when we used to sit in our towels on the front steps, shivering and comparing our wet footprints on the cement walk, the size of our feet until it grew dark and the fireflies started coming out, and the stars. And then we'd talk about time, time and space and marvel at it all, living on a ball revolving in a vast and empty expanse, and how far away the stars were, and how old the universe, and I'd make up some new scientific fact, I'd tell him I knew how to focus the rays of light coming from other planets and could see the past as

though it were on TV, and he'd believe me,
he'd believe every word.

EISENBAHNSTRASSE, and how different everything seemed with Artie suddenly there, occupying space and turning my studio into a displaced chunk of Staten Island that was becoming larger and larger each day. How he wore a pair of jeans once, a shirt once, throwing them onto the floor in the corner and the pile growing higher and higher until there were no more jeans, no more shirts in the suitcase, and my brother, having never been to a Laundromat, having never turned the dial on my mother's washing machine, having never left home, except once, when he ran away one day without any warning, and having nowhere to go, rode the ferry back and forth for an entire afternoon until a young man in a faded sweatshirt asked him if he needed a place to stay, who knows what he had in mind, but Artie never used to see these things. How, a few days later, I got a call from a friend, my former downstairs neighbor; a person was staying upstairs, he said, a young man with the same eyes as mine. He coaxed him down and put him on the phone, and strangely enough, it actually was my brother, who had just wound up in the same apartment upon leaving home as I had two or three years previously, crazy coincidence. I told him to come stay with us on Ninth Street and called my parents to tell them he was safe, and he eventually went back home and my mother gave up trying to talk sense into him and finally left him alone. Later, after I moved to Berlin, the snapshots of the family occasions I no longer took part in: christenings, birthday parties, my brother's graduation from the police academy, in uniform, and next to him his father, my father—was it really the same man?—with his hand around Artie's shoulder, proud that he had finally amounted to something decent. How I took him around the corner to see the parts of the Wall being dismantled, and how I tried to describe to him what it was like before, when the geography ended there, the map in the mind ended there and the grey zone began. And my brother's imagination was sparked all of a sudden: the sweep of history, the way the world can suddenly change, and I was wondering if the futon would dry by the end of the day, after having scrubbed it in the middle where the cat had urinated, out of jealousy, presumably, because I hadn't had an overnight guest for some time.

EISENBAHNSTRASSE. The trip we took up to Rügen, and all the little Trabants zipping past; the chug-chug of their two-stroke engines. The currency union had just gone into effect; the shops, closed down over the weekend for inventory and reopened now with new stock on the shelves, a new look of shy pride. A fabulous array with the four-color allure of marketing strategies still magically irresistible to those not yet inured; the sober disappointment when the effect on the monthly budget eventually manifested itself in hardship, but that came later. The emptiness that remained behind after my brother left, the feeling of instability; my clothes, hanging under the loft bed and looking as though they were waiting to be packed away, and how precarious the order on the desk suddenly seemed, everything with an air about it now as though it might pick up from one moment to the next and walk away. This living from rent to rent, commercial space, and if I had to leave, where would I go? All these paintings, too big to store in an ordinary apartment; *why don't you just sell them,* Artie asked, and I had to laugh; I didn't think of that. And all the paintings in the basement in the house on Staten Island; how he helped me carry them out of Ninth Street after you gave up the apartment, after you'd given up hope that I'd ever come back. And I, trembling as we maneuvered the huge canvases out of their storage in the front room and through the narrow ground floor apartment, their weight bearing down and threatening to fall on top of us; backing them one by one into the hallway, watch out for the door, watch out for the edge of the kitchen sink, the railing in the hallway, anything that might gash the back of a canvas and ruin it. How they were an inch too tall to get through the door; how we had to tilt them, feeding them diagonally through the opening and barely grazing the doorframe. And then they were outside, leaning against the building, everything I'd worked for during my last years in school, here, on the street. And in the meantime, the things I'd packed into plastic bags, old clothing, letters, receipts, strewn about the sidewalk, someone having ripped open the bags and rifled through them in the few minutes it took us to carry a painting outside. I stood and stared at my life, scattered about the sidewalk now, a piece of it carried here, a piece there, like bits of string to be woven into faraway nests. And the roll of drawings I'd leaned up against the garbage cans, gone, hanging, perhaps, in someone's apartment on the Lower East Side to this day, who knows. How we swept the sidewalk, spread out a sheet of plastic, and slowly lowered one of the biggest paintings down onto the cracked cement. I pried out the staples, removed the stretcher, and laid a cardboard roll onto the back of the canvas, as delicate now as a mammoth animal whose skeleton had been extracted clean as a fish. How we began rolling it, Artie at one end and I at the other, and how I heard the paint begin to crack. How we rolled it a little further, taking care not to let it stray to either side, and then I heard another crack, and then another, and how I had no choice but to continue, rolling it slowly, inch by inch, a crack here, a crack there, barely audible. We eventually packed everything onto the truck and tied the canvases I'd left on the stretchers to keep them from toppling over. And they'd been in the basement now for how many years, keeping me awake at night, and how I longed for everything to be in one place again, my bed and my dresser and the lamp on top of one of Grandma's crocheted doilies, with the piano in the living room and the World Book Encyclopedia in the book case, everything in its place, there, where it used to be, when the objects in the house had been there forever, would remain there forever, every picture on the wall, every worn-out piece of furniture, locked up and safe in one place.

I CLOSE MY EYES and imagine what it would be like to have lost you. A vast, dark space, and I, suspended, weightless, just as I always imagined it would be like to be an astronaut, lying in bed at night as a child with the pillow pulled down over my forehead and the blankets up over my chin, my imagined costume, my imagined equipment. And I would picture myself floating, and then I would really begin floating, and outer space was as warm and snug as the blankets I was tucked into, not this cold, barren feeling, this awful emptiness.

FIDICINSTRASSE and the neighbors upstairs, with a new baby born each year. I never knew if there were three or four, but one of them was always left screaming in the hallway while Sabine carried the others upstairs, why she always left this one particular child behind I never knew, but the little girl screamed and screamed and threw herself on the hallway floor and Frau Chran used to open her door and say what a crime it was to bring up a child like a gypsy. Once I went outside and picked her up and smoothed her tangled hair back from her face, where the tears had run tracks through the dirt and the snot had hardened into two patches of crust around the nostrils, and then Sabine came down and carried the child away in a huff of indignation. And the Mutter/Kind groups every afternoon, with seven or eight children racing around on tricycles over the bare wooden floors, dropping or flinging their wooden toys and hooting like cowboys tossing out lassos to round up the livestock; how the vibrations from the quaking ceiling spread to the walls and down them to the floorboards until everything in contact with them was vibrating. I used to take my book with me into the kitchen, then into the bathroom, looking for a quiet corner to read, but it was no use, the tricycles pedaled around the living room and the middle room upstairs, circling around and around the furniture while some branched off and tore down the hallway, looped around the children's room, and tore back. In the end, I would sit with my hands resting on the desk before me and feel the tremors move from my fingertips to my wrists and up to my elbows, vibrating with each new shock from above as the children pursued their relentless course. Or the trampoline: how the children used to jump up and down, up and down, and sometimes they lost their balance and landed on the floor upstairs with a loud thump, and then I could hear the metallic hum in the tiny springs of my desk lamp and the delicate sound of plaster dust falling from the small hole around the lamp hook in the ceiling, leaving a little white pile in the middle of the floor each time. And the other family across the courtyard, another Sabine with four children who hung her wash out to dry while her youngest child waddled around the littered courtyard in diapers, this Sabine whom we liked and who always said hello in her sturdy, cheerful way. How we used to hear her yelling from somewhere inside the bleak apartment, *I'm going to wind up in an insane asylum because of you kids!*—and how we never thought anything about it. But then she disappeared one day, and her husband began doing the shopping, carrying in the Aldi bags* and the crates of Fanta from the beverage wholesaler around the corner as the summer dragged on, and then another school year began, but there was still no sign of Sabine. And then I entered a copy shop one day somewhere in another part of town, and Sabine's husband emerged from behind the counter with a huge stack of inkjet paper and muttered a vague greeting as I stood there, frozen to the spot, because all of a sudden I wasn't sure if this was really Sabine's husband, this man I'd said hello to nearly every day for the past eight years, but always in passing, always in the courtyard, and here I was, seeing him for the first time out of context, as it were, and he looked somehow different without the Fanta, without the backdrop of discarded refrigerators and rows of rusty bicycles in the courtyard behind him, and I'm not at all sure that he recognized me, either. One day I passed Sabine walking down Fidicinstrasse on her way to the building, wrapped in a dark coat and looking smaller somehow, bent, walking rapidly with her eyes cast to the ground and peering up now and again with a furtive glance. I caught her eye and said hello, and she smiled an uncertain, almost apologetic smile; *what the hell has happened to you,* I wanted to cry out, *did you go nuts, Sabine, you've got to get out of that apartment, not a single ray of sunlight the whole day long,* I wanted to grab her by the arms and take her somewhere, but where. How we thought Sabine had come home, but then we saw her husband carrying in the soda, carrying in the Aldi bags as usual, and we never heard her voice from inside the apartment again, and her daughters started dressing more flamboyantly, hanging around the front of the building and hurling sultry looks through thick veils of mascara as the older boys from the block passed by and snickered.

* plastic shopping bags from a discount grocery store

FIDICINSTRASSE, and that mysterious ticking sound coming from somewhere inside the wall, like a hidden clock. And the crazy young man who lived with his mother, the way he cried out Hilfe, Hilfe, late at night, sometimes for hours, and always emphasizing the second syllable, always in the same sing-song rhythm, Hilfe, Hilfe, help, help. The first time I saw him through the hedge, on the other side of the street, walking backwards alongside his tiny white-haired mother, carrying an Aldi bag. The shock when I discovered, much later, that they lived on the other side of our bedroom wall. How it took on another quality, this incessant chant that had always been so unreal, as though from an entirely different world, an entirely different reality, yes, just on the other side of the wall. And the ticking sound, sometimes, sometimes not, and we would lie in bed and listen to it, wondering what it could be, this mysterious, irregular clock, could it be a machine, no, could it be the contractions of a beam, of a pipe. Sometimes, lying in bed awake, hours later, the cry would begin again, Hilfe, Hilfe, barely audible at first, then growing steadily louder, *Hilfe, Hilfe,* and always this emphasis on the second syllable, always this awful regularity. The first time I heard it, when can that have been, I jumped out of bed and ran first to one window, then to another; I thought of calling the police, I thought of running out into the street, but then I hesitated, the cry too much like a chant to be the cry of someone in sudden danger, in sudden need of help. This danger was ongoing, this need of help would never be met. Lying in bed, listening to his chant sometimes, in the dark, afraid, but of what, and wondering if you were asleep, wondering whether to wake you up.

FIDICINSTRASSE, and the suitcases standing in the kitchen waiting to be wheeled out over the courtyard's irregular pavement. The uneasy feeling in my stomach, checking to see if my ticket was still there, checking once again to see if my passport was still there, the keys to the luggage, the keys to the loft: What else might I need? And what if the suitcases are lost? So many airports, so many moments of arrival, of departure, taxi rides and cancelled flights and telephone calls to airline companies, and each time the tearful anxiety, each time my inability to get through to a living human being, only a recorded voice backed up by a choir in jubilant song. Struggling to comprehend which number I needed to press and somehow missing the cue each time, forced now to listen to the entirety of the customer service message, the music: once, twice, around and around as though on some bizarre carrousel, the background lyrics circling dizzyingly, maddeningly in my head, sung in a fervent falsetto ascending three octaves to a triumphant finale. And wasn't I always trying to imagine who these people were, these angels singing on high, this woman with her chummy, confiding tone, familiar somehow, and yet utterly unreal. Pressing the touch-tone telephone tightly to my ear, its buttons leaving a painful imprint in my cheek, then pulling the phone quickly away to *press one now, press two now,* and always afraid of missing some other, crucial piece of information in the process. Doubtful as to whether or not I'd properly understood and suddenly redirected to another recorded message—yet it was always the same song, begun at some other point in the melody, perhaps, but always the same celestial symphony, chopped into segmented sequences and pieced together again imperfectly, as though through some warp in time.

A SUDDEN RECOLLECTION the fol-
lowing day, and I am acutely aware of having
neglected to express what I'd set out to. I hear
myself begin, hear my words carry me off on a
tangent; and, as though my mind had reset the
warning signal for the next morning, all at once
I recall the precise moment when I embarked
on a final detour, failing to pronounce the most
important thing of all, registering a look of
momentary confusion on your face, and losing
the thread of my story.

KENT AVENUE, and the dense fog that settled over the city, muffling the millennium celebrations in a thick blanket of chilly mist. The party on North Tenth Street: holding my drink in my hand like the reins of an animal struggling to break away as I stood in the corner watching people dance. They don't know what they're revealing about themselves, I thought; they dance and imitate movements they've seen on TV, and they don't know what they're revealing about themselves. The Polish man who had been filling my glass with vodka an hour or two before, dancing now, as well; how he kept thrusting both arms high into the air as though he'd just won some kind of championship, turning around in half circles and addressing an invisible stadium of cheering fans, facing first one hemisphere, and then another. And I, standing there watching him, thinking about a movie I'd seen on a plane recently about two criminals who'd discovered a bug in the system and broke into the national security or some big financial base and punched something into a computer the moment the hour turned zero. Images of computer systems crashing, airplanes crashing, stock markets crashing, the total apocalyptic scenario drummed into the collective mind for weeks already. And then, the uneasy walk back along the waterfront, my hand clutching the keys in my pocket and my teeth chattering from the damp and the cold. And when I reached the building, all the people coming and going, laughing, reeling, all the taxis pulling up outside, all the bottles scattered around in the elevator, the hallway, the bathrooms, pools of spilled beer everywhere speckled with soggy confetti. How I visited a party first on the eleventh floor, and then on the ninth floor, and how I stood in a corner each time watching people dance. And how I eventually returned to my loft a flight below and opened a bottle of whiskey as the party raged on next door. A string of Christmas lights hanging from the windows and a fog so thick that it swallowed the skyline and bridges whole. I emptied the bottle and wandered next door, where the evening's amorous adventures were already in full swing, the flirts of a few hours before having tipped somewhat askew, with speech slurred and lipstick smudged and a drink spilling down a dress here and there. And my neighbor, the daughter of an American soldier and a Swabian Fräulein, dancing around in dizzy circles and throwing her arms around anyone she happened to bump into; how withdrawn she always was when I met her in the elevator with her bicycle helmet strapped under her chin, and how affectionate she became when she was drunk, trying out the few German words she knew and beaming at me for approval. I eventually wandered back home, pulled out the Christmas lights, and crawled into bed as the party dragged on next door, lying in the dark with the prospect of sleep seeming hopeless and gazing out onto the impenetrable fog, in which luminous orbs gathered around the streetlights like rumors around the unsuspecting. And how I fell asleep nonetheless, and then woke up a few hours later with my head pounding and a bitter taste on my tongue to discover that the sun had come up and the fog had lifted and everything was still there where it should be: the bridges, the towers, invincible and inevitable as morning.

KENT AVENUE. The naked space, the dazzling view. Plumbing running along the ceiling, windows across the entire front wall; the cement factory and the Brooklyn Navy Yard outside, and in the distance, the steady procession of lights moving over the Manhattan Bridge and up the FDR Drive. How I turned off all the lamps in the studio and sat in the dark, gazing out onto the city of my birth, of my mother's birth, my father's birth—and a grandmother's, a grandfather's, but that's where it ends, the trail becoming lost the moment it touches the shores of the old continent again. How I carried Grandma's armchair out of the basement where it had been sitting in the dark for twenty years, twenty-five years, and tied it to the trunk of my mother's car and drove it to Brooklyn; but that came later. I shook the cushion covering out the window, shook out the crumbs of foam, hardened after so many years and disintegrating; the beautifully inlaid zipper, that funny fabric with the stagecoaches on it, why is it that none of us ever learned to sew, there was once an entire slipcover for this chair that fit perfectly, with a stiff little ruffle at the bottom and piping around all the seams. I shook the cushion covering out the window and watched the orange-colored crumbs of aged foam become caught in a current of air blowing up from the river, hover, and drift to the ground far below, and then the cover itself slipped out of my hands and fell the eight stories to the street. And there it was, this slipcover with the stagecoach fabric in the middle of Kent Avenue, and then a truck ran over it, and then another; but that came later. And to think of this: Grandma sitting in her armchair crocheting all those years, upstairs, in the house on the other side of the harbor, before the fabric wore through, before her furniture was carried down to the basement and the first tenants moved in upstairs, in the middle of what used to be marshland, drained by the settling Dutch centuries ago. And to think of this: this building existing, this window existing all the while, waiting, the metal handle on the cast-iron window frame, here, now, before me, opened and closed by so many hands, for so many years, waiting for me, waiting for this moment, waiting for Grandma's chair and the orange crumbs of old foam, visible from the Brooklyn-Queens Expressway near the Flushing Avenue exit amidst a landscape of warehouses and water towers and scaffolding bearing huge neon signs. And now, sitting at this window with an undefined span of time ahead of me, six months, a year, and then I saw it for the first time, the power plant you worked in when we were little, before you were transferred to Kips Bay. You, and you. How is it that I didn't see it before, how is it that the name of the street didn't ring in my ears, Kent Avenue: the faraway place you went to every day, came home from every day, the mythical sound it once possessed, and only a word, the way you pronounced it; former times.

KENT AVENUE; the reduction of everything to the daily essentials: a bed, a desk, a sink, a gas stove, a refrigerator. An otherwise empty space, with a few pieces of clothing, a few books, my suitcases lined up beneath the plywood platform of the bed, these three massive suitcases on wheels. How Kati had paid Rigo's guys to seal the floor with epoxy, and how it never really adhered properly for some reason, and then, as more and more of it came loose from the cement, how it grew pale and milky, until it felt as though I were walking on a surface of brittle paper. And one day I started poking a hole into it, poking and poking until I finally peeled up an entire sheet, and then I turned it over to discover a perfect mold of the floor, a detailed imprint of the pitted cement surface. How I spent a month scrubbing the old oil stains and etching the cement with an acidic solution; how I applied a layer of weatherproof, and then a final coat of sealer, and how everybody thought I was crazy with my floor fetish, on my hands and knees for a month scraping and scrubbing and talking of nothing else. The reflections of the evening sun that wandered obliquely along the side wall, along the back wall, watery, wavy reflections cast through the older panes of glass and superimposing a grid of luminous orange trapezoids over the walls and the plaster casts I'd glued to them, small white hemispheres poured into an old diaphragm and left to harden. Everything I'd brought with me was stashed away in two metal cabinets, slide files and catalogues and documentation for the project I couldn't bring myself to continue working on; how smoothly the rolling drawers pulled out, and how final the sound of metal hitting metal when they closed. I used to stand in the empty space and imagine building a little half wall behind the gas stove, imagine installing a toilet so that I wouldn't have to walk to the end of the hall, but I never built the half wall, I never installed the toilet, I merely stood in the space, watching the light as it changed, gazing out of the window and dreaming as the evening reflections crept quietly across the wall and the last fiery fleck of sun finally disappeared behind the buildings.

Everyone in their own world, their own private universe, all these imaginary rooms and landscapes existing in people's minds, coexisting, colliding. Take a look around at the expressions on people's faces, at their faraway eyes: they're all seeing something that's not there, that woman sitting at the corner table with her cup of coffee growing cold, for example, staring at some fixed point in space before her, but at what, what does she see, nothing's there but empty space, an umbrella stand, a wall. And yet an entire scene is unfolding before her eyes, right now, visible to her and her alone, flickering bits of sunlight sparkling through brilliant green leaves, a hand reaching up to brush a strand of hair from a lover's face. Or that woman over there, the other one, can't you see by the look in her eyes that she's counting, adding something up in another one of life's ruthless calculations: the amount of time she needs to get to the grocery store and back, perhaps, or the number of times she's been betrayed.

KENT AVENUE; cleaning the greasy fingerprints of putty off the glass in the windows, sweeping the rubble from the narrow ledge beneath and watching it fall down below to the street. How it took some weeks before all the glass was cut and inserted into the gaps in the window front, sixty panes of glass, and all of them slightly different in size, three-eighths of an inch, or five-sixteenths, stacks of glass lined along the hallway floor with little slips of paper scotch-taped to each. How I bent down and brushed off the thin layer of sawdust and peered into their green iridescent space, their underwater kingdom. The sound of the trucks kept me awake at night those first few weeks, huge trucks parked downstairs in front of the entrance to Certified Lumber, with their refrigeration generators rumbling loudly and the drivers catching up on their sleep in the back, and I used to get up out of bed and gaze at the river, the skyline with its hundreds of thousands of twinkling lights, waiting for the moment when the first rays of morning light hit upon a particular façade and set it ablaze, long before the sun made its appearance on the horizon and a small group of scraggly men gathered on the corner, waiting for a man in a yarmulke to come out and choose among them if there was any loading work to do that day. How the center of reflection gradually shifted over the months, the early rays of sun illuminating first one building, and then another a week later, like a modern-day Stonehenge. And in the afternoon, sitting at my desk and gazing out the window at all these surfaces of stone and metal and glass, what a hostile environment, I caught myself thinking, hostile to human flesh, and the city took on a threatening character for me those first weeks; I thought I heard the sound of thousands upon thousands of feet trampling the weak and tired into the pavement like fallen leaves trodden into a muddy path. Buildings emitting invisible energy, countless waves of electromagnetic fields and signals crisscrossing and overlapping; how I had to squat on the floor in the corner of the loft to carry on a telephone conversation without picking up one of the radio stations transmitted from the antenna atop the World Trade Center, and how I began suspecting that even the metal fillings in my teeth were tuning into some wavelength or other, because they hurt the entire time I was there, but that came later.

KENT AVENUE, and the helicopters flying overhead on their way to the airport, and always directly over the building, every diplomat or head of state leaving the city of New York, directly overhead, within a stone's throw, so to speak. It would have been easy enough for them to land on the roof; it was broad and flat and higher than the rest of the buildings in the area. Imagine that, to walk up three flights of stairs to the roof, climb into a helicopter, and be off. Good morning, Mr. Arafat. How we sat up on the roof in the biting cold one night to watch the lunar eclipse, and how the moon disappeared behind a cloud; we sat huddled together in a huge coat waiting for the moon to reappear through a break in the clouds, waiting with our eyes fixed on a certain point in the sky, anxious that we'd miss it, and then it did appear, briefly, reddish brown and with a perfect silver ring around its circumference, and we watched it until it disappeared again, huddled in the old coat with the fur collar I bought for fifteen dollars around the corner, the coat you wore to Flora's dentist in Chinatown after lying in bed with a toothache the afternoon you arrived, the coat I posed as a bum in for my sister's daughters, curled up on the floor next to a garbage bin in the Staten Island Mall, motioning for my sister not to give me away, but that came later. *Hey, sweetheart, got a quarter to spare?* A brief moment of incredulous joy, and then, turning their faces away, embarrassment; an obvious miscalculation on my part. We pulled the coat tightly around us, holding the collar up against the stinging wind, thinking about how the precise moment of concurrence across all these millions of miles of space was a known quotient, as was the moment of the next eclipse and the one after that, as easy as a few billiard balls on a table. To perceive oneself as part of this perfect alignment, to feel the pull of the axis extending to the darkened moon and back behind the earth to the sun, as though they were suddenly closer somehow, as though one had come into the path of a huge and supremely watchful eye.

KENT AVENUE. The wrinkly spot on the hallway floor from the afternoon Lillian and I hung around talking, Lillian with her cell phone clipped to her hip pocket, taking a break from caulking the shower stall, and I leaning against the newly erected wall, wondering if the color of the floor hadn't turned out too pink. How I suddenly felt the hardened skin of the paint give way under my feet and shift slightly over a softer underlayer that hadn't yet quite dried through. And later, all the times I stood and gazed at the spot in the morning while waiting for Henry or André to emerge from the bathroom in a cloud of steam, clutching my towel and shampoo and mumbling *good morning* as I looked up from this wrinkly scar in the floor which had been mopped over countless times since, each time leaving behind a fine skein of dirt that settled into the filigree pattern of wrinkles. And each time I watched the shreds of a dream wander along the pattern's paths until the last trace of sleep was lost, and later, after having learned the morning schedules of the floor's inhabitants, I began getting up to shower just as the sun was making its first appearance over Brooklyn, looking a bit squashed on the horizon, like an overripe orange that had fallen off a table. Every time I walked through the hallway, my eyes were drawn to the spot, and although it was nothing more than an inconsequential testimony to a casual conversation, I followed the gradual progress of its darkening with a strange sense of foreboding, as though there had been something malignant imbedded in that moment, in the image of Lillian's good-natured smile, in the sound of the coin-operated dryer at the end of the hallway, the clack-clack of a zipper hitting against the inside of the turning drum, or the smell of warm, damp laundry. I cleaned the lint screen every other night, carefully lifting the soft, thick blanket from the plastic netting and stashing it away in one of the metal file cabinets with a peculiar feeling of indiscretion, a peculiar feeling of having stolen something, but what, it was nothing more than the collective lint of the eighth floor's inhabitants. And later, I rolled the lint into tiny balls, dipped them into diluted glue, and left them to dry in front of the window. How I made little stockpiles of these grey and bluish balls veined with individual threads of various colors and a hair here and there, miniature weightless cannonballs that made a hollow sound when I tapped them on the edge of the table, and how this feeling of having stolen something wouldn't go away, or not entirely, and I turned the little balls around in my fingers, thinking of all the secrets hidden away inside them and wondering what it meant to be a thief.

You, AND you. Sitting in the old Peugeot; you suddenly turned to ask me a question, and the face of another appeared, there, in place of yours, vivid and fleeting. And the twilight, a deep blue luminescence unwilling to relinquish its hold on the day and lingering for hours. And sometimes an eerie orange light at sundown, when the faces of passers-by seemed to glow from within, burning in their very being. This other face, a momentary hallucination: another you, for years, but then one day no more.

NINTH STREET, and the smell of chicken roasting in the oven. How you loved to cook, acquiring a kind of vanity about it and boasting about your recipes. And only a year before, you were still adding black pepper and chopped chives to a can of Campbell's mushroom cream soup and calling that cooking, but what did I know, I was still eating potato chips and Baby Ruths and hardly knew how to boil an egg. The mattress we bought in the foam shop on Houston Street; what were we sleeping on before, was it the bed I took with me when I left home, Grossmutter's four-poster—I can't recall. And her trunk, stowed away under the heavy oak bureau perched on four tin cans to accommodate the trunk's height: Laura used to marvel at the economy of space, as though those four tomato cans were somehow a mark of genius. A tiny apartment crowded with canvases and old furniture, like some kind of dilapidated trousseau; you used to put on the Rolling Stones and sing along off-key, that small, coy curl forming around your mouth. I can almost see you now, sitting here by the window, looking out over the roofs of buildings and at Alexanderplatz far in the distance, reading a letter you'd written to me twenty years ago and seized with an urgent desire to answer an appeal I'd never really understood before: how to go back in time and comfort you, appear the very moment you needed me most. I was always dragging something home that I'd found on the street, old windows, pieces of plywood, screwing them into the canvases and painting over them. The luscious feeling of Prussian blue oil paint sinking into the crevices between the wicker threads of a discarded chair seat; cadmium red over a smooth square of embossed tin from an old ceiling. The streets were an endless, abundant source of material, and our lives were lying mute before us, and I wonder what I would have thought if I'd have known anything of what was to come, would I have wanted to go through it all, just by the sounds of things, would I be able to seduce this earlier version of myself with an embellished account, emphasizing the glories, the adventures, leaving out the disappointment, the defeat. Sometimes we climbed the six flights to the roof to gaze at the tops of the elm trees in the park and into the upper stories of the Christodora Building, which was still in ruins back then, hadn't yet been converted into luxury condominiums with a uniformed doorman downstairs; the windows were broken and the interiors lay waste, long before the mayor posted a cop on every corner and eventually drove the drugs further out to the fringes, before he cleaned up Times Square and I was still picking Kerstin up after work and she'd emerge from one of the cabins in fishnet stockings and tremendous high-heeled shoes of the kind transvestites bought in special shops, size twelve, but that came later. Kerstin wasn't a transvestite, just a long-legged painting student from Berlin putting herself through school by working in a peep show in New York each summer with a bushy blond wig, a black bra I'd lent her, and keen blue eyes brimming with derision for her desperate customers. And Kerstin would explain to me how important it was to retain control, to call the shots, and I would marvel at this, and at my own incapacity for deciphering power relations in a given situation, but Kerstin was impervious, Kerstin would stare at her own reflection in the two-way mirror, lightly running her fingers under the elastic of her dessou and licking the tips, indifferent to the individual invisible on the other side of the glass, who was, in a sense, left to his own devices, reduced to seeking satisfaction in a small airless cabin that remained, despite the frequent sponge-downs undertaken by the cleaning personnel, sticky with the stray ejaculate of countless customers before him, slipping folded dollar bills through a little slit while Kerstin held her breasts up to the glass like juicy fruits and curled her tongue over her upper lip. I suppose some of them had to pay seven or eight dollars to achieve relief, and others had to fork over twelve or even fifteen, the money in one hand and their uncooperative member in the other, and I used to hang around the small lobby waiting for Kerstin to wash the rouge off her cheeks and change back into her street clothes as I chatted with the other women, who were topless and garish, but friendly, making an honest living, I soon learned, feeding and clothing their kids in the absence of husbands or fathers, or powerless to break away from boozing, beating, desperate men. There was a fat, affable guy named Ronny who made sure the customers didn't harass the women and stopped them at the door if they didn't pay; it never occurred to me that he probably carried a gun. And then one day Ronny pulled me aside and offered me one of the early shifts, *you can make good money, kid, and nobody will ever lay a hand on you.* I'll think about it, my smile seemed to say to him, but I knew that I couldn't ever count on the kind of infinite anonymity Kerstin had found in New York and which made the steady stream of men's faces somehow unreal for her. And I knew that, improbable as it might have seemed, and while attempting to derive at least some measure of gratification in the process, someone I'd gone to high school with, for instance, would one day be sitting on the other side of glass, indiscernible to me, yet observing me, observing me intently, unable to put his finger on it at first, perhaps, but eventually, inevitably recognizing me as the awkward, brainy girl who'd tutored him in differential equations and whom he'd noticed stealing glances at him now and again from the other side of the classroom when she thought he wasn't looking.

NINTH STREET; how Dibbs came by the day we moved in to give us an estimate on window gates, but then we built large plywood shutters instead, bolting the hinges deep into the wall and cutting a two-by-four to size for a barricade. And Phil, standing outside on the sidewalk, showing us how easy it was to slip a knife in between the shutters and shimmy the stud up out of its metal braces at either side. And so we glued a plywood lip over the edge and screwed it into place, yet we were surrounded by stories of prowlers drilling into locks, prowlers in running shoes scaling the walls of narrow air shafts, climbing through windows on the third floor, the fourth floor, they can break in any-where if they're clever enough, desperate enough. And all the more easily on the ground floor, it would have been child's play to break into our apartment, although we had nothing to steal, only an old stereo that wouldn't have brought in more than fifty bucks. How Walter and I sometimes hung around the Chinese fast-food on Twenty-third Street, waiting for someone to throw out an unfinished lunch; how we quickly moved towards the bin, one of us fishing the Styrofoam container deftly out of the garbage while the other studied a plastic laminated menu on the Formica counter. And then we'd share the leftover snow peas on rice, soggy with soy sauce someone else had squeezed out of a little plastic package, and then Walter got worms, and that was the end of that. The mirrors we hung up everywhere to make the place seem larger; the Modigliani print taped to the refrigerator and the milk crates with art books stacked on top, books that became infested with cockroaches when I went away the following summer and granted them a reprieve in what had been a bitter ongoing battle. And then the fronts were left unguarded and gradually dissolved, lines of boric acid I'd sprinkled along the backs of the cupboard shelves and behind the stove for the roaches to scurry over and carry back to their nests, that adhered to their bellies and suffocated them and maybe some of their offspring, as well, but that came later. It was essential to lay the trap regularly, it was the only way of keeping them in check; how cold and murderous one can become, how engaged in another creature's systematic demise. And after I returned, how I reached up for a book on Cézanne one afternoon and they streamed out in all directions, up my bare arm and across the wall, having multiplied in my absence, nesting in the books and feeding on the glue of the bindings and leaving behind weightless piles of empty larvae shells, thousands upon thousands of tiny diaphanous cocoons.

NINTH STREET. The windows facing the air shaft, blackened with years of soot, and I, crouching on the windowsill, my arm reaching as far as it could go to smear a wet rag over the outside glass as dirty suds streamed down my arm and up my sleeve in the process. The long, white smears of bird excrement streaking the brick façade; the sound of dishes clinking, pigeons cooing, a baby crying, all mixed together and resonating in the enclosed space. And a few feet below, at the bottom of the shaft, a pile of rubbish of uncertain depth that Virgil once vanished into after taking an exploratory jump, but we didn't know that yet, she just disappeared one day and we assumed she'd squeezed through a small hole in the window grating facing the street. How it took weeks to find her, crouched in a remote corner of the basement, thinned down to the bone and with whiskers full of spider webs and too dazed to respond to her name, although we must have been within inches of her several times, shining the flashlight into dark, filthy corners and finally giving up and going back upstairs, but that came later. And how did we wind up with so many dogs, it was crazy to have any animals at all in such a tiny apartment, yet you'd taken yours with you when you moved out and I'd taken mine as well, but then I thought the better of it and brought her back to Staten Island, and your mother stopped babysitting Bobby's kids and started sleeping at home again, and so you hauled Butchie back up to the Bronx and we only had the cat and Red, who was already so old that he didn't do much more than lie curled up in an armchair all day and snore. And then I was out walking Red in the park one evening and he disappeared all of a sudden, and so I ran home and told you to come, and then we hurried back to look for him, calling his name and searching in the bushes, in the playground, in every dark spot beyond the streetlights' reach, and then it started to rain, and we climbed over park benches and iron fences, jiggling his leash and calling out his name as the rain grew progressively heavier, calling and calling, but no Red, only a little black pup that appeared out of the bushes now and again, its wet fur plastered flat to its trembling body. And how long did we search, an hour, two hours, and every so often the black pup would appear, its eyes flashing in the dark, and skitter away again. And eventually we gave up hope; Red was gone, we decided, and then the puppy suddenly appeared again out of the underbrush, its tail tucked between its legs, and we tried to coax it to come, but only frightened it away, and then we finally made up our minds to go home when we noticed it following after us, and so we'd left the apartment that day with a dog, and returned home with a dog, but a different dog, a wet, hungry little dog who collapsed in my arms as I dried his drenched fur with a towel, breathing out a deep, exhausted sigh. And so we decided to keep him, what else could we do, and every day we came home to a new scene of disaster, the dog having chewed the armchair to shreds in our absence, or a ten-pack of toilet paper, his black figure surrounded by a sea of shredded white, his tail thumping rapidly against his haunches, an uncontrollable chewer he was, and we later learned that some kid in the neighborhood had kept him chained to a railing for a few months before he grew bored of having a pet and let him loose in the park, and so we mourned Red and at the same time set about taming this jittery dog with a history of abuse and a long, pink tongue that streamed behind him as he raced around the park, barking at all the slower, fatter dogs, and even the bigger, meaner dogs, scampering up to them and yapping into their faces and getting them angry, inciting them to chase after him, and before we knew it there would be a pack of dogs of all shapes and sizes, howling and yelping and woofing up a mayhem that could be heard for blocks, scrambling in large circles around the park with the black pup in the lead, his lean black silhouette and his long pink tongue trailing behind him. Red was an old hound, hunchbacked and rickety in the bones, and we told ourselves that he'd sensed his time had come until we got a call a week or so later from a lady who ran a boutique on the Upper West Side and who'd traced us through the license tag attached to his collar. A dog that could barely stand up straight, and he'd somehow made it all the way uptown, dodging every oncoming car, every taxi in midtown Manhattan. And you got on the First Avenue bus to pick him up and then you stopped by the studio on the way back downtown, and that was when I realized how poor Red's vision had become, because at first he didn't seem to recognize me, but then I called his name and all at once his ears perked up and his eyes grew bright and he came hobbling in my direction, his bony haunches slightly askew and his crooked tail thumping weakly against one flank. And then we brought him back to the apartment, and the pup capered up to him and licked his ear, and Red snapped at him and climbed into his chair and went to sleep. And in the days that followed, Red became increasingly evasive, and no matter how much extra attention we tried lavishing on him, trying to prove that this was nothing more than an unfortunate misunderstanding, and that he hadn't, contrary to appearance, been replaced, he refused to respond to the usual affections—the scratch behind the ear, the morsel of chopped meat now and again—and so for a few weeks he growled at the pup whenever the opportunity presented itself, and the pup grew afraid of him and kept out of his way, which was nearly impossible in such a tiny apartment, but then Red disappeared again one day, and this time it was for good, and we never got another telephone call, and we never found out where he chose to finally lie down and die.

IS THAT HOW IT WAS, that moment, that story, or was it all very different? Do I still remember the expression on your face that day, do I still see the flicker of light across your cheek and the shadow of my own profile on the wall behind you? Someone opening a third-floor window, a reflection of the late afternoon sun, lower on the horizon now and flaring up in one brief, blinding flash; your chair at an angle mirroring that of the window to the sun. I glance up and see two hands shake a towel out into the courtyard below; then the towel disappears and a hand pulls the window shut as a flash of reflected sunlight illuminates your face once more. And this time I can see the worn-out hem of the curtain, a silhouette of individual frayed threads appear briefly alongside my own shadow on the wall behind you, and then vanish again. But perhaps it wasn't like this at all, perhaps it was all very different, and my mind is reaching back and rearranging things, filling things in, and the figure seated in the chair is someone I've begun to reinvent, and the figure casting the shadow on the wall is a person I have long since ceased to know.

You, and you. And the next day, as though a charm had been broken, our fairy-tale garments restored to the rags they were before, our magical world having vanished at the tap of a wand and the impatient sounds of a new day pressing in from all sides; a working day. I can hear the dull rumble of a refrigeration generator outside; downstairs is a driveway leading to the back entrance of a grocery store around the block. A truck has pulled up to the curb to unload. I get up from the desk to close the window and the telephone rings; when I pick up the receiver and hear your voice at the other end of the line, I understand with a dull ache that I've been dreaming again. But weren't you under the same spell as I—and don't you long to find your way back into that garden, to lie upon a bed of flowers and hear me breathe sweet, hushed words into your ear. How you once appeared through the crowd in Fanelli's and sat down wordlessly on the stool beside me; how you began sketching a floor plan on the back of a sheet of letterhead

paper left over from the recommendation Jeanne
had had me type that afternoon. I watched your
hand, studied the small play of muscles in your
forearm as you puzzled over a way to conjure a
little more space out of a tiny apartment. Finally
you drew a meandering line along the bottom
edge of the page and laid down the pen; I slid off
my stool and headed for the bathroom. Mike was
still alive back then, presiding over things from
the back of the bar, weightless and shriveled and
already well over eighty, throwing out anyone
who started a brawl and cashing checks for his
regular customers. I closed the door and pulled
the latch and stared at my own reflection in
the mirror; I unbuckled my belt and undid the
zipper, and all at once I found my fingers tracing the sporadic line of hairs below my navel,
slipping lightly downwards beneath the elastic
band. I thought of your ugly little paintings
piled up with paint, muddy blobs that had begun
to dry on the palette, that had already formed
a skin and that you'd scraped off and smeared

onto the canvas. Sometimes there'd be a tiny dot of red or yellow in the middle of a wrinkly field of thick oil paint, one moment of hope in a murky darkness. We'd meet and talk about these things, taking them apart and trying to get at the essence of our own respective forms of expression; I hadn't realized how much I desired you. I pulled the chain and returned to the bar and laid my hand on your shoulder, and then all at once I saw a head of bright orange hair: Jeanne was approaching, and my first reaction was to turn around, to hide. I'd been sitting in her office only a few hours previously, waiting for her to finish a telephone call and sign the recommendation; I'd watched her place the receiver back on the hook and make a few notes in the calendar spread out on the desk before her, asking *where were we* as I tried to collect my thoughts and the telephone rang once more. How many times had I sat in this office, how many times had she tossed help my way, although I never really understood why, because

Jeanne only responded well to people who could stride into her office with an air of entitlement and demand something. Years later I would remind you of this evening, sitting at the bar as you folded your napkin cautiously into triangles and told me that you'd like to share a bed with me one day, years later, after we'd already done so several times and you sat cross-legged in the tangle of blankets next to me, holding my face as I trembled in silence.

NINTH STREET; Michael at the door. Three in the morning, four in the morning, at first a quiet knock, and then louder, and finally, if we were already sound asleep, an insistent rattling against the doorknob, a pounding with the back of a fist or a shoe until I finally heard the muffled sound of my name cried out in a lugubrious slur. And I would stumble out of bed and open the door to Michael's desperate, drunken figure surrounded by an aureole of harsh fluorescent light shining from behind. What's the matter, what's happened, and Michael, close to tears, eyes widened in profound sadness: *my only friend.* I would make him a cup of coffee and we'd sit whispering in the kitchen while you continued to sleep in the next room. Michael was always talking about poetry, about wanting to die, but not yet, *not yet,* he would intone; the raised eyebrows, the index finger pointing skywards in admonishment. And sometimes Michael would read me a poem he'd written, and the skin on my scalp would tingle with emotion, and eventually he was right, I was his only friend, after he'd been sleeping on the floors of everyone he knew on a rotating basis, borrowing fresh underwear and wearing out their good will and hospitality. Michael was incapable of making a home for himself, of turning back a blanket and putting himself to bed, of buying a quart of milk and leaving it in the refrigerator for next morning's coffee. Take care of me, or I'll give myself up, I'll let myself perish. Michael's eyes studying me, probing the boundaries of my character. You'd turn me out, you'd forsake me? And where is he today, is he still the same person I remember, sitting in our kitchen smoking thoughtfully as long worms of ash dropped to the floor; lighting a fresh cigarette from the one about to go out, like a continuous flame. *That air you loved, heard in the blaze of an afternoon mid wheat and horizon, feet paced like a second hand / that air you loved.*

NINTH STREET. Sitting at the table in front of the window one morning, watching the sanitation workers empty the garbage cans into the truck and then throw them back onto the sidewalk as the truck inched on to the next building. Sometimes some of the cans would roll out into the street, where cars had to steer around them until one of us ran outside and dragged them back in, the hollow aluminum cylinders rumbling like heavy drums. I went outside and lined them up in front of the building again, picking up the scattered refuse and balancing the smashed lids on top like absurd hats. It was June, not yet seven in the morning and already hot and humid, already there was a thick smell of decay hanging in the air; I was listening to the annual reading of Ulysses on the radio, Scylla and Charybdis. You were still sleeping in the middle room, and I felt an overwhelming aggression rise up within, a trapped rage. We'd taken over Phil's job while he was away, free rent for mopping the hallway, for sweeping the sidewalk and checking the boiler in the basement, and then I left that summer and Bobby helped you with the job, but that came later. I gazed through the metal grate at the sidewalk outside, thinking of Phil's fifth-floor apartment and how the sun flooded the tiny rooms, making them seem twice as high, twice as spacious as our own. He was always so good at building things, a drop table attached to the wall of his tiny kitchen, a narrow column of shelves built into a doorway, and always so well done, always such a perfect utilization of space, like the hook in the ceiling he hung his bicycle on, screwed far into the beams above the layer of plaster and secure enough to bear real weight. Later, after I returned to New York, sitting at the same window again, gazing out onto the row of battered garbage cans, each one carrying the number of the building painted in a large and clumsy hand that dripped at the end of each brushstroke, listening to the sound of the steam hissing from the radiator and trying to draw. And then one day Phil came back from Japan and went through the tools he'd lent us, checking them off the list he'd compiled before he'd left, and suddenly the ratchet set was missing, the drill, Bobby'd sold it all, and we had to go out and buy new tools to replace them, with both of us broke and Bobby nowhere to be found. And when I went upstairs and knocked on his door, Phil appeared in a silk robe and handed me a pair of bamboo thongs, having redesigned his apartment in Japanese style, with a straw tatami on the floor and a delicate porcelain tea set carefully arranged on a low table. He'd shaved his thick black beard, revealing a pockmarked jaw, a long skinny neck, and I hardly recognized him; his head seemed to be half its former size. Roughly hewn wooden busts were resting on the floor in the back room as though submerged to the waist, figures with necks craning and arms pushing against the ground, struggling to free themselves from an impending engorgement. How strange the sculptures looked when Phil lifted them one by one and carried them into the corner; how light they seemed with their contact to the ground suddenly broken and their missing limbs no longer projecting into the imaginary space below the floor. And a year or two later, looking out of the window of Alba's apartment on Wilhelmshavenerstrasse, I jumped at the sight of a pair of jeans hanging outside to dry, dangling on a hanger from an upstairs window and turning slowly from side to side, because Laura had just told me that Phil was dead, that his Japanese girlfriend had found his limp body hanging from the bicycle hook, and that she couldn't lift him out of the noose and had to cut him down with an electric drill, the only thing she could find that was capable of severing the thick rope, the drill we'd bought to replace the one that Bobby'd sold to the second hand dealer on First Avenue.

HOW TO GO BACK IN TIME; one would have to subtract everything that has come after, shed the skins that have accumulated since: peel them off one by one and forget them. To undo all that has occurred, to have found oneself in none of these situations, to lose entire parts of oneself; to forget. To disappear, to undo oneself. And when my mind carries me back, it is as another.

NINTH STREET; how I went upstairs and knocked on Laura's door and began to cry. Another official letter from the academy, full of incomprehensible words, many of which were capitalized and extended halfway across the page: perilous words, monstrous words, and I, understanding nearly no German, trying to decipher the content with a pocket dictionary. Laura invited me in and sat me down and told me that I didn't have to go, that I could just as well stay in New York. And later that day, wandering around the city with all senses alert to the concurrence of things: a paper coffee cup tossed from a passing truck, rolling along in the gutter and coming to a halt; a dog trotting up to a lamppost and raising its leg to urinate while a trickle of coffee leaked out through the cup's lid and carved a path through the dust nearby. One thin trickle slowly snaking its way around a cigarette butt, a bottle cap, about to be met by the river of steaming urine. I gazed at the projected point of intersection and saw a slip of paper lying on the ground; I bent down and snatched it up a moment before the two streams crossed paths and the larger artery flooded into the smaller one, coffee mixing with dog urine. And then the surface tension became exceeded by other forces and the swelling waterway spilled its banks and flooded encircled areas previously enjoying island status. I looked down and studied the writing on the slip of paper, an address of three ones, and I had to think of this concatenation of three, the truck, the dog, the unknown individual, three factors mysteriously interconnected in an equation meant for me and me alone. And I thought of the hour, the minute before, and all three having no notion of their impending link: the person whose coffee had grown bitter, or cold; the dog, sniffing its way down a curb, accumulating the content, formulating the exact phrasing of the olfactory message it would presently leave behind; someone examining the contents of his pockets to count out his loose change: is it enough for a pack of cigarettes, or does he have to break a larger bill— and suddenly finding the slip of paper that had already served its purpose and tossing it into a garbage bin, and missing. But perhaps it fell out of his pocket accidentally, perhaps the moment was yet to come when it would fulfill an important function, and the person was stopping and searching his pockets that very moment, several blocks away, trying to find the slip of paper with a certain address written on it, searching first one pocket, and then another: and what will this lead to, and what will be lost as a consequence? Holding it now in my hand, it seemed as though I had been addressed in a language of happenstance, as though a voice were whispering a cryptic message into the din of occurrence, and I nearly became dizzy when I realized that I was the only person who had perceived it, and yet I understood nothing, nothing at all.

NINTH STREET, and your sleeping body on the bed in the middle room. Months when we barely spoke to one another, endless summer months I spent waiting, working, scraping together the money to leave you. How I walked across town every morning to save the subway fare, one long walk from Avenue B to Hudson Street; how I always arrived with my blouse wet from perspiration and with blisters on my feet from the cheap plastic shoes I wore. And always holes in the toes of my nylons, always the anxious hope that the runs wouldn't spread above the tops of my shoes by the end of the working day. A handbag with a sandwich wrapped in aluminum foil and the instamatic camera I carried around with me like a precious secret, anticipating the moment when I would find what I was waiting for and press the little red button, once each day, one photograph each day. Rust stains spreading out from a spigot and patterns of erosion on a building's façade, and sometimes just garbage on the street or a swirl of oil in a dirty puddle. On some days I found nothing at all, having waited too long and the light having grown too dim, but I always took the picture anyway, even though the film couldn't record much more than a murky blur; a lesser day. And how difficult it was to get those blank days developed; how the laboratories automatically skipped over them, and I had to make a special request each time, had to explain that I wanted these worthless pictures developed too, and in the end I had to pay for a hand development because the machines couldn't be made to print the underexposed negatives, but that came later. Searching for clues, searching for myself, for patterns that seemed to carry some kind of meaning, to contain something that might lead me to who I am. And the job, paste-ups and mechanicals, blurred vision and headaches from the fluorescent light, and at lunch time, sitting on a bench outside, eating the sandwich I'd brought with me and adding up the hours I'd worked, always double-checking the multiplication, always worried about making a mistake. Calculation upon calculation in ballpoint pen on a napkin, this is how much I will have earned by August, this much by the end of September, this much every hour, every second. I'd finish my lunch and take a walk over to the jetties on the riverfront, scrutinizing every surface along the way, the cracks in the asphalt, the scraps of litter along the curb, or what had once been a winding snake of spilled paint on a sidewalk of granite stones, long since dried and hardened, the fluid line fragmented now, the stones having been dug up at some point to fix a gas pipe, a water pipe, and then replaced, fit back together again, but in a different order, cutting the flow into segments of equal length going first this way and then that; how happy these things made me. Sometimes I worked late into the evening and called the driving service, company policy extending to anyone who worked overtime, and thus even to me, and I would sit in the back of a chauffeured limousine and let myself be driven back to our apartment, thinking about the absurdity of this misplaced luxury and wondering what the driver might be thinking, a young woman with oil paint under her finger-nails, hair a wild mess, and a heart torn between staying with you and leaving, staying and leaving.

How I passed through Tompkins Square one morning on the way to work and saw you across the park with a cup of coffee and a newspaper, letting the dog out for a run. You'd pulled on your clothes and had left the apartment by the time I got out of bed, yet seeing you now on the other side of the park with the leather leash dangling at your side, sipping your coffee and squinting into the hazy morning glare, it suddenly seemed as though I were seeing you from another time, the sunlight shining on your hair, your unmistakable gait as distant and inaccessible as the past. I imagined that I could walk up to you and utter your name, and you wouldn't see, wouldn't hear me. We never spoke of my imminent departure. Later, in the airport, how I told you not to wait for me, and watched the imprint of my cruelty appear on your countenance. How I turned around and walked towards the gate, feeling your gaze from behind; how I laid my hand luggage onto the security belt, passed through the metal detector, and hesitated at the other side, but the machine hadn't beeped, my baggage contained nothing of interest, and the airport personnel simply waved me on, as I was already beginning to obstruct the smooth flow of hurried passengers.

A WORD, A GESTURE my mind keeps circling around, something left unsaid, a flicker of misunderstanding appearing in someone's eye—and nothing having been done, nothing having been said to stop the process of estrangement in its tracks. I see the error and let it occur, fascinated by a detail, or a mechanism. A loose knot of rope affixed to a jetty unwinds, and I sit and gaze at the intricacy of the movement, surprised at its improbability and forgetting for a moment the boat that is already drifting away, irretrievably.

BEDFORD AVENUE. Sitting at the desk, gazing at the old photographs I'd brought back with me to Brooklyn: Grossmutter on the roof of the building in the Bronx, leaning against a low brick wall and resting her large hands on her lap; you and I in a coin-operated picture booth in Asbury Park, the date written on the back in ballpoint pen: May 20th, 1962. You were wearing a plaid cotton jacket and a cap and holding me up to face the lens, and I was clinging to your neck, turned halfway around towards the camera, but I didn't know that, all I saw was a pane of glass and perhaps our own murky reflection, and I was gazing at it with a mixture of curiosity and mistrust, unwilling to let go of your collar to take a closer look. I studied your face, beaming broadly in your perfect new dentures, and then I went and fetched the ladder and pulled the box of photographs down from the top shelf of the bookcase to look for one of the house when it was new, but that came later. The cement sidewalks had just been poured and the grass seed sown, and someone had strung cord around the perimeter for protection, tying it to little sticks wedged into the dirt. There was nothing else around, not a single tree, a single bush; the houses across the street hadn't yet been built, the houses in the back hadn't yet been built, only ours and the house next door, a kind of odd twin with two front doors and a wider front porch, and this quality of being similar but not quite identical made it look particularly suspicious, particularly alien. And there you were in your plaid jacket with the Brownie camera hanging around your neck, and there I was, an infant in Grandma's arms. The baby carriage was parked to the side, on the fresh cement, and a leg of a pair of trousers hanging from the clothesline was visible above it; I was about to turn the photograph around to look at the date on the back when I suddenly noticed your strange smile. So that was when you lost your teeth, I thought, toothless before the age of forty; they were extracted while we were moving into the new house, weren't they, but why did they have to pull them all, surely they weren't all bad. But perhaps it would have been too expensive to have a root canal done, a gold crown, and perhaps the dentist had simply recommended a more economical solution, because all the money had gone into the down payment on the house, the mortgage. October 1961; my child is the same age now as I was then; you were the same age then as I am now, and it took years for the sewers to be dug, and the basements on the block kept flooding every summer, because they were built on what had once been marshland; and I suddenly had to think of how an entire row of poplar trees fell one year in a heavy rain, and of the frog I tried to keep in the backyard and the little pond I dug for him, and the fireflies we caught on summer nights to collect their eerie light in pickle jars with holes punched in the caps to let in the air and tufts of plucked grass arranged at the bottom.

BEDFORD AVENUE; the long dark hallway packed high along one side with lumber dragged in from the street. How the walls were open from behind, revealing a haphazard collection of screws that caught on to the plastic bag each time I dragged the garbage to the back stairway, ripping it open and causing the cat litter to spill out all over the floor; how I had to stuff everything into another bag and sweep up the mess before carrying it down to the dumpster on Metropolitan Avenue. And then someone new moved into the loft behind and began pushing the litter box in front of our door, to let us know how disgusting they found it, no doubt, but what could I do if Bruce kept an extra litter box in the hallway? Now and again, a call came in for Bruce, a bit of work here or there, light construction, substitute teaching, that was what the neighbor in the adjacent loft did for money. I told them Bruce was traveling, took down the telephone numbers, and promised to pass the messages on, but Bruce never called, and his neighbor didn't have a number for him, either, and I wondered what it must have been like between them, back when they were still friends and not just co-signers on a lease, when they took on the space and drew up their plans and set to work at building their artists' community. Bruce's neighbor used to come home from work in a foul mood and his dogs would begin barking in excited commotion; he was always yelling at them to shut up, stomping through the hallway and rattling the keys as the dogs worked themselves up to a deafening pitch, and he'd shout at them to shut up, will you just *shut up?*, I always heard him yelling from the other side of the trembling wall. And how the dogs kept barking anyway, out of sheer joy, from the sound of things, locked up in a dark space all day in the unbearable heat and aware that their chance for escape was at hand, finally a bit of fresh air, finally a bit of movement, barking and barking, even after he began whipping them with a leather leash, joyful, even if it meant no more than a short walk down the block and back, with the chain pulling at their necks nearly the whole way, panting from the heat and the excitement. I used to be able to tell the sound of his walk from the moment he entered the floor, and I would tense up, anticipating the plodding step, the desperate joy of these trapped creatures, the shouting and cursing, the sound of the metal chain hitting against the aluminum studs on the other side of the wall as I sat at the table under the skylight, cutting a picture out of the newspaper. I put down the scissors and studied the page spread out before me. Lots of Arafats, smiling Arafats printed on posters held aloft by a small crowd of Palestinian youths. Two, three boys no older than ten, eagerly holding their Arafat posters out in front of them, one of them biting his lip in an effort to hold it high and steady, and another holding two Arafats at once, his slender chest thrust out in a boastful pose. And a smaller boy, his eyebrows drawn and serious, the poster in

his hands hanging somewhat slack, an Arafat
to his left, to his right, two Arafats behind him,
and all of these Arafat heads markedly larger
in size than the boys' heads or the heads of the
young men behind them. And then, to imagine
the scene with only the boys and the men, but
no Arafats, this scene of a crowd of smiling
Arafats without Arafat, without any Arafats
at all, only the three boys and the man to the
right, the two behind, a small crowd, animated
expressions frozen by a camera, but no Arafat,
take away the Arafats or substitute them with
balloons, for instance, everybody could be holding a balloon, the boastful boy could be holding
two. First a crowd of Arafats, a hyper-Arafat,
whereas in reality there was no Arafat, but only
printed paper. How photographs of human
heads look just as flat in print as the printed
images of human heads beside them. One afternoon I came back along Bedford Avenue and
stopped at the corner in front of the building,
where Bruce's neighbor was standing on the

sidewalk embracing a young woman, both of them tearfully embracing one another, and I heard them as they promised to write, cupping each other's faces tenderly in their hands while a car with a Minnesota license plate was idling at the curb, and I could hardly connect this tearful, tender farewell with the scuffle and the foul language and the unloved dogs, and I stood, stunned and staring at this intimate scene that had nothing to do with me, that it was an indiscretion to be staring at in this way at all, repressing a violent urge to hurl myself onto these two figures and embrace them both.

BEDFORD AVENUE, and the grey cat that bullied his way through the door every time we let the black cat in for dinner. How he always went after the brown cat, chasing her and then trapping her in a corner, and how she used to cry out in fear each time. We had to get the broom and scare him away, you covering one side and I the other, an unbelievably tough cat, afraid of nothing and always managing to slip through. How he found a way to break in through the wire mesh protecting the windows that looked out onto the roof, and how we found a staple gun in Bruce's tool cupboard and stapled the mesh back into the wood, but the cat undid it again every night, scratching at the wire for hours until he finally broke through.

A LOOK, NOTHING MORE, and a quiet avalanche is set into motion, a wordless disaster. How can anyone presume to know what another person is thinking, feeling. I can only report on the outer signs, the recurrent phenomena. But I know you, I say, and see the indignation rise up within, the rage.

KENT AVENUE, and the Christmas cards
I sent out with my telephone number, my first
New York number in years. How I finally went
to visit you and discovered the water kettle my
sister gave us one year, how long ago was that,
there, on your gas stove, in a new apartment,
surrounded by a life I no longer knew anything
about. And Virgil, a kitten in our time, now
grown old and poor of sight. She would have
suffocated in the refrigerator once if we hadn't
come back home again a few minutes later for
some reason or other; how did she get locked
inside, we never could figure it out. She used
to nestle into Red's groin and suck on a pimple
there, and he would snarl and try to kick her
away, but he was so old and stiff in the joints
that he eventually gave up and fell back to sleep
with a low growl. And Sasha, her kitten, one of
the five products of coupling her with Cub, the
wild grey tomcat Walter and Laura had taken
in. We'd watched the births, all five of them,
and then we laid a blanket in a cardboard box

for Virgil and her kittens, but she carried them out of the box and into our bed anyway, one by one, and one by one we took them out and gingerly laid them back into the box next to the radiator and propped the canvases up between the front and middle rooms, there being no doors to close, and Virgil picked each kitten up by the neck and scaled the canvases to the top and then climbed down to the other side and dragged each kitten back into our bed, one by one, and so we finally gave up and slept with five kittens on the pillow between us, what else could we do. Do you remember? And the wine glasses, the water glasses you took from our apartment after I left for Berlin, did you know that I stole them from a restaurant I worked in uptown, checking coats? One by one over a course of months, this restaurant in the theater district with aspiring actresses waiting on the martini lunch crowd, I remember one of them running after a group of businessmen too drunk to leave a tip, asking in a shrill voice if there

had been anything wrong with the service.
And I, before the news of the scholarship
arrived, with my German book, pronouncing
the foreign words, whispering them into the
coats surrounding me in the tiny booth, *Herr
und Frau Fuchs sitzen im Wohnzimmer und
trinken Kaffee,* * a free lunch and a dollar a coat.
The water glasses, the wine glasses, the mattress,
the kettle, these things from our life together,
but how can she know that, how can she know
when she utters the cat's name how many days
I spent narrowing the list down until it was the
only one to remain. *Lasciate ogni speranza.*

---

* *Mr. and Mrs. Fuchs are sitting in the living room, drinking
coffee.*

KENT AVENUE, and the evening my brother came by after target practice, carrying a large duffel bag; how he kept casting careful looks over his shoulder, how he wouldn't let the bag out of his sight until I stowed it under the bed and locked the door to the loft and we climbed the stairs to the roof. The lights were just beginning to go on all over the city; we watched a tugboat push a barge under the bridge as a faint breeze blew off the river and the evening sky darkened. *Risk your life, and what do you get for it? One unlucky thing happens, and they stab you in the back, and then they don't know you anymore, fifteen years down the drain just like that, three kids and a mortgage.* And I had to think of the weapons downstairs, and the party going on next door, and I had to think of how many violent deaths were lying dormant in these things, in a round of bullets, like so many unlived lives within embryos, and how easy it would be to pull a trigger, and how they were itching to be used, to be aimed arbitrarily into a crowd, or turned around, bang, without even thinking.

KENT AVENUE; walking past the 99¢ stores up Metropolitan Avenue to catch the J train; traveling out to my sister's for Christmas. The lush synthetic tree, the tinsel, the piles of presents underneath; the video camera following everyone around as though it were an autonomous being independent of the brother-in-law, the nephew holding it. The way the older people grew stiff and silent, offering a quick wave of a hand from the couch or chair they were sitting on and then turning away again while the younger ones automatically broke into a kind of easy, spontaneous narration: Hi everyone, it's Christmas, there's lasagne and antipasti on the table, and Grandma's grating the Parmesan, say hello, Grandma. One of the children pulled a videotape down from the bookshelf, and all of a sudden, superimposed upon this occasion, a previous one appeared, with more or less the same people, with a few years in between, a birthday party, a Christmas gathering not very different from this one, too much food and the blare of a television mixing with the sound of the stereo from the kid's bedroom and an electric guitar trying to get the heavy metal sound right; one Christmas superimposed upon another like a mirror with a time delay. And the children were laughing at themselves, laughing and pointing and poking each other in fun, yet there was a vague sense of discomfort beneath their gaiety, something uneasy in their eyes; do they notice it, I wonder, as they watch themselves clowning around on the television screen in last year's clothes, an inch or two shorter, their voices a bit higher, making fun of each other, but watching, watching intently. And then the camera swerved for a moment, sweeping past the children kneeling in a sea of presents and wrapping paper and ribbons, and then, unexpectedly, I caught a glimpse of you, smiling, sitting on the couch and smiling, and then, just as quickly, you were gone again, the camera swerved away again, away from the couch and back to the children holding up their presents and making goofy faces, and you were sitting there next to them, just beyond the camera's frame, invisible, leaving me gripping the arms of the dining room chair and stung, as though I had been slapped in the face.

SEATED AT YOUR DESK, finishing the last of your wine, when the bottle suddenly flew out of my hand and struck the opposite wall with a loud thump, shattering into a spray of tiny glass shards. And earlier, gazing into your face, my hand suddenly flying out to strike it, an impulse so precipitous that I searched my memory for a forewarning which might have preceded it, finding nothing, not even a vaguely felt desire to hurt.

KENT AVENUE; how I hadn't done anything I'd set out to do in New York, how I'd called off the exhibition and worked on the book instead, and sometimes I would go to Laura's and sit around with her drinking beer and listening to records in this apartment that hadn't changed much over the years. And how many times had I stayed there, sleeping on a futon and feeling the floorboards shift beneath me any time someone crossed the room in the apartment next door. Once, I flew back a day before Laura was scheduled to return to New York and stayed overnight as the guest of a German girl who'd sublet the apartment for the summer and who confessed how little she liked staying there as she helped me carry my luggage back to the building, *what a cramped apartment, so run-down, so hot and stuffy,* and we climbed the three flights of stairs as the familiar smell of insecticide and rat poison told me I was home. As it turned out, Annette hated Laura's apartment; she'd tacked up lengths of cloth to conceal the walls and had painted the floor a bright cerulean blue, leaving brush marks around the bottom edges of all the furniture, but Annette didn't care, she was concerned with obliterating as much of the apartment as possible for the length of her stay, that was all. How transformed everything seemed, like entering a tiny harem, one cave of bright billowing silk leading into another. And then Cub peered around the corner of the fabric, gave a cry and jumped up onto my lap, and Annette looked on in horror, having spent much of the summer fighting the urge to kick the cats out altogether and make up a story to tell Laura, so unbearable did she find the animals, so filthy, *I could have killed them myself,* she'd said as we'd reached the third floor, it's perverse to keep animals in a place like this. Cub sat on my lap, watching Annette intently and purring under my stroking hand, and I was glad to have found at least one thing that recognized me in these bizarre surroundings when Girl suddenly appeared from the bedroom, glanced in my direction, and broke into a smooth, precise leap, and then both cats were on my lap, purring and arching their backs as hairs flew all over the place, and Annette looked as though she were repressing an urge to scream, but she gathered her wits and made a prim excuse, a date she'd nearly forgotten, and I could see she was angry, that it was too late to go back on her offer, and that she would have to put up with me on her last evening, but all I could think of was sleep: Laura will be back tomorrow, I thought, and then we'll tear down all this fabric and return the apartment to the way it was before, and I lay there on a mattress on the floor, a denizen in a foreign cave, and fell into a deep sleep with cockroaches crawling over me, because Annette hadn't cleaned much at all that summer, and we found the empty cocoons of countless generations of larvae behind the fabric when we pulled it down, but that came later.

KENT AVENUE, and the night Walter drove me back to the building after we'd spent the afternoon drinking whiskey and looking at drawings. Dark circles carefully layered in graphite; words revolving concentrically from the center outwards, dreams Walter had etched into the paper with a sharp point, leaving a fine white imprint in the penciled surface. Paolo's motorcycle suit hanging in Walter's closet like a leather ghost, its elbows and knees still bent from years of use; drawings that resembled maps of the night sky. And what else did he inherit from his friend? I held one of the drawings in my hands and slowly turned it around, following the circular path of a sentence, barely legible in a field of deep black. *Snow, ice, everywhere. Trying to make my way through ... a meteorite or bomb plunges into the snow in the distance, creating a tidal wave that we run from, managing to stay just ahead of it. Multi-colored grubs are offered for food. Seems natural, and I reach for one, waking up.*

An image of an overturned stool, of Paolo lying on the floor with the needle still in his arm. Shadows lengthening across the kitchen wall, roommates drifting in and out, lingering for a few moments in the hallway mirror before disappearing upstairs or pulling the screen door shut behind them. And how many different people have lived in this house? Do you remember the earthworms in Billy's box of topsoil on the kitchen floor, his neighborhood garden projects? I never saw him emaciated, never saw him wasting away with glassy eyes turned towards the window in an apathetic stare. I picked up another drawing to read the spiraling words. *I'm in class and the new teacher tells us to strip off our clothes, down to our underwear. She has difficulty writing on the blackboard and keeps running out of room, so she continues writing on blackboards that stretch out of the window and across the countryside. We have to run across fields and wade through creeks to copy down the notes she is writing.* Billy's easy, learned manner, pronouncing the Latin terms of plants and organisms I'd never heard of: a Garden of Eden, right here in a Brooklyn backyard. Later, sitting in Walter's old Pontiac on Kent Avenue, and then it got late and I crossed the street and waved good-bye as he made a U-turn and headed back for Powers Street. How Walter had driven me to Soho to pick up my things from the gallery the day before: a year of gathering everything in, everything that had made its way out into the world, work left over from exhibitions, scattered in different countries, stored in flat files, in painting racks, some of it easy to get back, but much of it tiresome and arduous. How cruel we were, strolling casually around the gallery before we finally picked up the boxes left by the door and pressed the elevator button. *I am wiping away the dust and grime from a stained glass window. Emotion wells up in my chest on the verge of exploding. People are watching and I am revealing something to them ...* A continuous formation of alliances, betrayal of promises, the self reinvented again and again and again. No good-byes, only a brief glance around, holding the elevator open before letting the metal doors slide shut behind me. Around and around, the sentences circle around and around. Letter by letter, word by word, around and around and around. *I am shot in the back of the head while seated in a restaurant. I've had this dream once before—I remember the sensation of pain on the left side of my head and then I taste blood and slowly lose consciousness. I know the gunman ... I convince him that it's okay to kill me, even though he's reluctant. He circles behind my chair several times ... Finally I raise my arms to signal that I'm prepared, and I almost welcome death.*

ON THE J TRAIN BACK TO MARCY AVENUE, waiting for the building to appear through the metal maze of the bridge's construction, this battered castle on the waterfront visible from far and wide. How the evening sun cast sharp stripes over people's faces, deep golden stripes that illuminated the skin as though a light were burning from within and that danced rapidly to the rhythm of the clattering subway; strange how immutable and absolute a moment can seem in such fiery transience. And the Puerto Rican girls with their switchblades, clowning around and playing with their knives amicably as the sun caught hold of the metal again and again like a sudden flame. Put that thing away, one of them said, suppressing a giggle; you look like a typical Puerto Rican. Laughter. People slouched in their seats and napping or standing with an arm clutching the overhead bar, rocking gently from side to side and reading the Daily News. The billboard the train always passed as it pulled into the station: DIAL 1-800-COP-SHOT, with a jagged red smear running diagonally through the second O, designed to resemble the view-finder of a handgun or a target. And the sun shining on the carefully groomed Hasidic women with their babies, their ladylike hats pinned into their sheitlen and shining in a brilliant glow that cast everything into sharp relief, rendering each individual hair clearly discernible. I close my eyes and find myself submerged in a radiant space the color of my own blood, reflected through the translucent membranes of my eyelids; I open them again and wonder how long the last moment of a life can last, can it stretch out to infinity, I wonder, can the soul become immobilized, suspended in a never-ending phase of transition? A disaster lurking at every step, at every turn; each new moment harboring a plethora of catastrophe waiting to occur. I walk along the edge of a subway platform as a train pulls into the station, and I know that it is a matter of inches separating me from annihilation, or a mere flick of the wrist as I drive along the highway dividing line. Every day, the thousand little things that can go wrong—my station could arrive unexpectedly, and in grabbing the belongings on my lap and hurrying to get off the train, I could trip over the strap of my bag and a leg could become wedged in the chasm between train and platform as the subway doors close— a thousand little things to watch out for, their devastating consequences; one moment of negligence, disaster waiting to occur at any moment.

TO BE NO MORE than this one physical entity carrying its memory around inside a fragile skull, like an egg on a spoon. My entire existence dependent upon keeping this soft and delicate matter intact, keeping it properly fed, keeping it from springing a leak and losing its precious fluid, this body which will be outlasted by everything I see around me, everything I touch: the chair I am sitting in, the paper I am writing this on, none of it is as ephemeral as I. The blood that pulses through my veins, my heart beating, all these metabolic processes in infinitesimal concurrence, all these cells transporting this or that, like billions of busy ants in a huge ant megalopolis of systems and structures and functions. And the one particular weakness inherent in the machinery is in all likelihood manifest even now; one particular curve of an artery, conducive to a minimal acceleration in sedimentary accretion, for instance. The precise moment the gradual narrowing of a vessel will cease to allow free flow at a given degree of viscosity is a calculable quotient, perhaps even now. Yet I am still alive: my heart beats, my eyes see, I am still ensconced in visceral experience, and the ants continue hurrying to and fro, to and fro.

BEDFORD AVENUE: the imprint your sweat left behind in the varnish of the piano seat; the collection of newspaper photographs tacked to the wall. The 92nd St. Y, and the times I went swimming that summer while you sat playing the piano we rented from the shop in Ludlow St. in your undershirt, your underpants. The whirlpool bath, the pounding sound of people practicing a form of martial arts above the locker room. The dance performance of elementary school children down below in the gym, on the basketball court; how I watched them through the window of the exercise room built into the gallery above, struggling with a machine designed to simulate the climbing of stairs. And the parents standing against the wall, some of them carrying bouquets of flowers, what did a two-month membership cost, I don't remember anymore, but we were living on six dollars a day, three of them spent on subway tokens each time I went uptown. How we hid our traveler's checks in tin foil in the freezer.

BEDFORD AVENUE, and the day Tamara called to tell us that Fidicinstrasse was infested with fleas. She turned the key in the lock and entered the apartment with the aim of watering the plants, she said, and found herself under siege from all sides. She didn't know what it was at first; stung by a multitude of tiny piercing pains and only realizing the cause after she was already standing knee-deep in a sea of jumping black specks. And I, sitting at the table cutting pictures out of the newspaper, wondering who you were talking to. An image of a small crowd before me: old women in head scarves, old men in woolen skullcaps, arms held high in the air, mouths open in mid-cry. Each of the women is holding a framed photograph aloft, six pictures suspended at various angles like buoys bouncing on agitated waters, six young men, some of them gazing stiffly into the camera's lens, some of them dreamily, some in half profile, some of them mere boys. Three are wearing suits and ties, one is dressed in a shirt unbuttoned at the neck, one in a military uniform, and to the right is the photograph of a man standing on one knee, with a tight-fitting beret pulled down to a slant and arms holding a Kalashnikov against a bared, flocculent chest. His eyes are frozen in the blind stare of the arranged pose; wall-to-wall carpeting and the edge of a television, a sofa are visible in the background. A photograph transplanted within another photograph, one time inside another, and in the background, flowers spilling over the edges of balconies, a terrace with a sheet of corrugated plastic serving as a sunroof; someone trying to grow a few tomatoes, perhaps. From a utility pole, electrical wires stretching in broad curves to the buildings lining the street, filled now with an excited crowd and their cries, arrested on film and forever silent, like the handmade sign held high on the crowd's periphery and erased by the glare of the sun. I take a closer look, trying to guess at the printed words, but all I can see are the indecipherable remains of single letters, formless blobs vanishing into the dots of the offset screen. I can hear them chanting, see them shaking their arms to the rhythm of their chanting. Some of the hands are gesturing, with the thumb and two middle fingers drawn together and the other two sticking out like the ears of an animal in a child's shadow game. *See, it's just a rabbit, there's nothing to be afraid of, my love, watch the rabbit's mouth move, the rabbit isn't afraid of the dark, is he?* Hands that fed, that diapered, that soaped and scrubbed, that ironed the shirts the young men are wearing. That brushed their jackets, stroked their hair, that lifted a linen cloth, making a sign now for their fallen sons, death to Öçalan, death to Öçalan. And you, on the telephone with Tamara, fleas; absurd. There was talk of calling in an exterminator; in the absence of a host, we were later told, fleas lie dormant. In anticipation of the host's return, however, they multiply at an accelerated rate.

AND ANOTHER PHOTOGRAPH: a group of men divided in two, figures frozen in a multitude of poses and expressions. Mouths half open in mid-jeer, mid-shout, jaws hanging loose or thrust forwards, teeth exposed behind taut lips, eyes rigid with fury, darting in apprehension. And a multitude of arms, bare or in sleeves pushed up to the elbows, gesticulating, grappling, converging towards the center of the picture, arms reaching into the camera frame, cropped on the left and right, holding an object aloft at the center of the photograph: an imposing gilt frame containing the painted portrait of an ethnic Chinese millionaire. His expression is attentive and dignified, his eyes, having gazed into the eyes of the portrait's painter, are gazing into the camera; behind him, in the distance, is his Indonesian home. A window front in a brick façade, drapes pulled partially open, revealing an interior in the midst of being torn apart; muddy shoes and bare feet tracking in the dirt and envy over expensive carpets and parquet floors, furniture being flung outside where lush trees and carefully trimmed shrubs frame the plundering mob. And the painted man, equal in size to the figures in the photograph and just as real, or rather just as flat on the printed page, wearing a dark suit and tie and posing beside an ornate chair, held aloft by six arms and a man with a balled fist, caught in mid-jump, mid-strike, and the painted man suspended, curiously unperturbed, his reserved gaze a magnet, a reservoir of calm in the eye of a storm. And in the foreground, a man in a baseball cap and a flannel shirt about to hurl a porcelain vase to the ground, where cords from electrical appliances smashed beyond recognition are snaking along the littered patio. An object is lying beside him, an overturned typewriter perhaps, its uncertain contours vanishing into the dots of the offset screen. In the background, several men are looking away from the camera, towards the door of the house, where the marauders are hauling out their booty; one man is smiling broadly into the camera, and another is casting an anxious glance over his shoulder. And the portrait, centered in the photograph, hovering before the camera's lens a moment before its annihilation, appearing as though it were imbedded securely in the pandemonium, strangely immutable and still, the portrait's subject impervious to the impending danger, inaccessible in his painted universe and safe. And a man standing behind it, concealed by the large frame and visible only from the waist down, his feet in rubber thongs, black pants cut off below the knee, two legs jutting out from underneath the canvas, like an extension of the millionaire's body, one moment of concurrence between the raging mob and their effigy, the millionaire having apparently fled just in the nick of time.

THE MOTHS THAT BEGAN NESTING
in the orange peels in the studio; how I didn't
notice it at first, a bag of halved peels in a plastic
bag, drying out in the corner near the radiator.
And one day I took them out and arranged them
on the desk, filled their hardened shells with a
mixture of plaster and glue, and painted them
over in white oil paint, leaving only the fine
edge of the peel and the dot of the navel free.
And every few days I painted them in another
layer of white, the soft hairs of the brush
gliding over their rippled surface, and then
I discovered a hole the size of a pin, and then
another, and I only realized the peels were
infested after a tiny yellow worm curled onto
the paintbrush one day, all these shriveled white
cups with little brown nipples and an invisible
proliferation of wriggling larvae underneath
the surface, burrowing miniature tunnels
through the plaster fillings. And what didn't
I try to kill them off, suffocating them in a pot
of turpentine, leaving them out in the sun to

perish, setting traps with the scent of a sex hormone meant to lure the male moths into its sticky clutches, but they were indestructible, weren't they, although some of them eventually resettled into the boxes of catalogues on the shelves, their orange peel paradise having become somewhat less than ideal. And then we moved one year and a few of the studio boxes were relocated to the new apartment, and now, after how many generations, a thin yellow worm occasionally crawls up the wall and I gaze at it in alarm, astonished at this tenacity, this will to live.

Eisenbahnstrasse, and the queues of East Berliners waiting for their "greeting money," a hundred marks a head, compliments of the government of the Federal Republic of Germany. Lines all the way up Köpenicker-strasse, Muskauerstrasse, snaking out from every bank in the neighborhood and stretching for blocks, wrapping around corners. People standing closely together, waiting in line quietly, impassively, shuffling a few steps forward now and again and nudging their belongings along with the toes of their soft-soled vinyl shoes, identical red and blue plaid tote bags packed full with thermoses and sandwiches wrapped in wax paper: people evidently accustomed to waiting. And now, their minds firmly set upon feeling some hard western cash in their hands, their own currency having grown somehow silly, with its lightweight aluminum coins and dwindling exchange value: how bitter to have worked an entire life for this very money and to witness it becoming suddenly invalid, ludicrous, an entire system, an entire country rendered invalid and ludicrous, practically overnight. I crossed the street, still hearing the sound of my mother's voice on the telephone, struggling with the medical details of your failing kidneys, these two spent organs steadily leaking toxic juices into your bloodstream. I closed my eyes and everything was strangely invisible, strangely empty, a black tunnel in a fun house with creatures jumping out of hidden corners, their faces briefly lit from below the chin with a flashlight flicked on, flicked off, and vanishing into nothingness. Later, after bringing your journals back to Berlin, I would set about decoding your cryptic shorthand, trespassing the successive chambers of your clandestine self until I was finally able to locate the day you'd been told to prepare yourself for the inevitable, the "Big K," as you'd dubbed it, the total renal wipeout. I pictured how you must have jotted this information down in one of the hand-made desk calendars you'd drawn with a ruler in a yellow spiral notebook, the receipt of purchase scotch-taped to the inside back cover, monitoring your body's demise and speaking to no one about it, but that came later. I opened the door to the drugstore and walked down a brightly lit aisle as an array of deodorants and shower gels streamed past to either side; I tried to remember what it was I'd needed to buy. I found myself slipping a bottle of shampoo into my bag, and I was so surprised that I stopped and looked around to see if anyone was watching, when all at once I felt a flush of anger rush over me; I don't want to fly to New York now, you can't die now, my life has been in shambles for so long, and now I've finally renovated a loft with the first real grant I've ever gotten, and I'm just getting started, *and when are you going to get a real job,* I hear you saying, because it was nothing more than a handout for you, wasn't it, money from the legacy of a painter whose works I'd often gone to see at the Museum of Modern Art on the "pay as you wish" days—the crowded

days—and to you it was charity. *Oh, Daddy.*
What was this anger, and why did the fear only
creep up the next day, on the plane, when I had
no way of knowing if you'd still be alive by the
time I arrived, but that came later. I walked up
to the register to pay for the dishwashing liquid
and the kindling wood in my shopping cart;
I tucked the change away, zipped my wallet
shut, and was heading for the door when a
large hand suddenly took firm hold of my
arm. Come this way, please. *You know, I don't
even know why I did it,* I said to the under-
cover guard, following him to the back of the
store as he pointed at the two-way mirrors
lining the walls to either side. I waited for the
police to arrive and take down my name and
address; I was admonished never to enter the
store again as I stammered out a confused
apology. Later, at the funeral, people would be
ogling me as though I were some kind of celeb-
rity; Berlin was the very place the world's eyes
were on, right that very moment, and I had just

181

arrived, still fresh with the aura of history in the making. I felt giddy, as though something incredibly funny had just occurred, and I imagined them all chiseling away at me, breaking off small, authentic chips, but that came later. A few neighbors arrived; one of the men from next door, where two Stanleys and two Wandas and a police officer named Jim lived, who used to reveal the most opulent cache of fireworks we'd ever seen at sundown each Fourth of July, like an overgrown child hoarding a stash of toys and firing them off into the wee hours of the morning. *Goddamn corrupt,* you used to say. *They're required by law to turn the stuff in, and what does he do? Typical Irish cop—swiped it away from a bunch of kids.* One of the Stanleys was approaching to offer condolences, and I felt a wave of dizziness come over me; he held out his hand, and although I felt deeply moved, it occurred to me that he might have been motivated by a sheer sense of morbid curiosity. I reached for his cheek and planted a wet kiss on his neck instead in a spasm of motor control gone momentarily awry; I drew back and gazed at this man with his long stringy hair combed over his scalp to cover his bald spot, who had slept and woken each morning with his unshaven cheek lying on a pillow a mere four yards from my own, who had walked down the same street to the same bus stop as I had, without exchanging a single word, a single glance with any of us, every day for years. How strange we always found these neighbors, and how quiet they were in comparison to our own sloppy, tumultuous household, their shades drawn and not the slightest sound, the tiniest peep, only once every so often, a sudden cheer, a round of applause from behind a Venetian blind, the two Stanleys apparently sports fans of some kind, but it was hard to imagine of what: it never took place during the football season, the baseball season, didn't concur with the hockey championship, the World Cup; perhaps it was some alien game they were cheering on, played by extraterrestrials on another planet. The line in the cement separating our driveway from theirs; how it always felt as though I were doing something dangerous when I hurried across it to retrieve a stray ball. Two children grew up in that house and we never got to know them; they were taught to walk looking straight ahead, taught never to say *good afternoon* or to engage in eye contact with anyone. And later, Mrs. Tobiassen came to pay her respects as well, and reported in a cheerful voice that had resisted the Staten Island twang and had stubbornly clung to its Norwegian color for decades that she and her husband were taking the greatest care of themselves, the *greatest care,* she stressed, to make sure that this—and she pointed at the casket with an index finger angled coyly, as though to tickle a small furry animal—*this* wouldn't ever happen to *them.*

AND THE NEXT DAY, how I met Aunt Emma at the Staten Island Ferry terminal and drove her back to the house, Aunt Emma chain-smoking the whole way and I drinking in the vowels, the faintly nasal pronunciation, this voice that sounded so much like your own, that contained an entire generation, an entire lost world within it. And back at the house, Aunt Emma looking for an ashtray, and I, searching the kitchen drawers and finding a hairbrush filled with a tangled ball of dyed hair and a pair of dentures, but no ashtray, searching the kitchen cabinets crowded with bottles of ground oregano and basil and prescription vials, my mother's blood pressure medicine, my mother's pain killers, and everything sticky with greasy fingerprints, but no ashtray, not a single ashtray in the house. And then Aunt Emma wandering into the kitchen with a lit cigarette and a hand cupped underneath to keep the ashes from falling to the floor, and my mother commenting to no one in particular that she didn't want to have that kind of stink around her house, around the food, and the plates and plates of cold cuts: ham, roast beef, provolone; the smell of coffee dripping through a machine and boxes of store-bought crumb cake and doughnuts stacked up on the kitchen counter. Aunt Emma wasn't hungry, and so I suggested we go out for some fresh air; she threw her coat over her shoulders and we left the house and walked to the funeral home as she smoked one cigarette after the next in thoughtful silence. We were about to cross the parking lot when I looked up for the first time and discovered a group of hearses lined up on the gravel, shiny black limousines reflecting the branches overhead in their flawless surfaces, and then I saw that the funeral home beyond them had doubled in size, that a second story had been added on top; strange that I hadn't noticed it the day before. We walked toward the entrance with the small stones crunching under our feet and entered a crowded lobby looking onto four individual parlors with a wake being conducted in each. I peered into one of them and saw an elaborate wooden coffin; the upper part of the lid stood open, exposing the powdered and coiffed corpse of a middle-aged woman lying on white satin, with a string of rosary beads draped around her manicured hands. I quickly looked away. It crossed my mind that I'd read somewhere about a scandal, a corpse that had only been groomed above the waist; someone must have considered it a waste of time to dress the rest of the body, concealed as it was by the lower half of the casket lid. *What you don't know can't hurt you.* We walked on and entered the room where my father had been laid out in a sea of flowers and his best suit and a pair of shoes with the date of purchase written inside in ballpoint pen, an idiosyncrasy of his, where the last of his brothers and sisters would soon be walking up to the coffin one by one to pay their respects, where Aunt Lulu, who could hardly walk anymore, would cry out *Goodbye Artie!* from her chair and everyone in the room would fall silent.

Later, I wandered outside and into the lobby, furnished with a number of stiff chairs whose gilt arms and legs curved out from underneath the velvet upholstery and dimmed by heavy brocade curtains gathered to either side in two broad, majestic sweeps and held in place by braided cords with golden tassels, wondering what kind of historical style this was supposed to represent, here in the middle of Staten Island, across the street from a Burger King and a K-Mart. I sat down on one of the chairs next to an ashtray, a slender aluminum cylinder containing a collection of snubbed-out cigarette butts, their heads submerged in sand like a flock of odd birds, I thought, and lit a cigarette. And a moment later, an old man sat down next to me and introduced himself; he used to work with my father, he said. A fine man. I nodded politely and stared at the carpet; my eyes followed the imitation Persian pattern up to the heel of someone's shoe and stopped. He was a good father, I answered and turned to look at him.

He was always talking about you, the man resumed, how his daughter did this, how his daughter did that, you were his pride and joy, did you know that? I studied the lines in his face, this man whom I had never met before, yet who had known some other part of you, the part that left home for work each day, hours before we got up for school, that sat down to lunch each day with a ham sandwich, maybe, or scrambled eggs on a roll, the two of you in your identical grey overalls, your orange hard hats resting on the floor beneath the table, a half an hour for lunch and a newspaper opened to the sports page, the baseball scores. The man stared ahead for a few more moments, his gentle face lost in thought, and then he turned to me and said that he was going to pay his respects one last time before going home. I thanked him and gave him my hand, and then I watched him walk away, struggling to remember his name, realizing I hadn't heard him properly, hadn't really understood his name at all, but maybe my mother will know, one of my father's closest friends from work, surely my mother will know, and then I saw him pass the parlor where my father's body was lying in state, walk on to another door at the far end of the lobby, and shake the hand of a stranger standing outside, having come to attend somebody else's funeral, and having unwittingly consoled the daughter of the wrong deceased.

ALL OF A SUDDEN I turned and asked Uncle Louie about Pippi, in a whisper, whether he was still alive, whether I could visit him, and Louie stared ahead at the casket for some time and then he wrote the address of the sanatorium on a slip of paper and pressed it into my hand with a ten-dollar bill. Take him out to lunch at the diner down the block and buy him a few packs of cigarettes with whatever's left over, he said, and then he stood up and walked away. And when I did make the trip to Far Rockaway a few days later and stepped out into a vigorous ocean wind, I decided to buy the cigarettes first, and then I buried my face in my coat as my scarf whipped about my face, one block, two blocks in the bright, cold sun. I signed in at the front desk; there was a kind of community room to one side with a television installed above the door, where its control knobs were well out of reach, and then a nurse's aide appeared and led me into a small room with an old man lying in full dress on a narrow bed. *There's someone here*

to see you, Joseph. The old man on the bed
didn't respond. *Wouldn't you like to get up
and say hello to your guest, Joseph?* He's dead,
I thought, can't you see he's dead? But then
the old man obediently rolled over and pushed
himself up into a sitting position. The aide
smiled at me and left the room, and I stood
next to the bed and didn't know what to say.
I'm your niece, I began. The old man looked up
at me impassively. Would you like to go for
a walk? He stood up slowly and shuffled out
of the room with his head bent low. I didn't
know what to do, and so I followed. I just
arrived from Berlin, I said as I caught up with
him, and he stopped, his eyes growing wide.
No kidding, he answered; it seemed he'd been
watching the news coverage, hordes of bewil-
dered East Berliners passing checkpoints in
tiny cars; hordes of ecstatic West Berliners
cheering them on. I'm Artie's daughter, do you
remember your brother, I asked, but I wasn't
sure if he understood. I offered him the pack

of cigarettes, and his face lit up; I watched him peel away the cellophane wrapper and light one carefully, sucking the smoke deeply into his lungs. He's dead; he passed away last week, I said, but Pippi didn't answer, he merely lit up one cigarette after the next, smoking each one down to the filter and then crushing it under his shoe. Now and again, he got up from his chair and shuffled across the room, and then I followed and took a seat beside him. He seemed to have forgotten all about me as he sat there smoking thoughtfully, and at some point, I stopped following him every time he changed his seat. There was a commercial on television: a happy family in a beautiful home; a trim, manicured mother holding something behind her back and smiling knowingly into the camera. *Just pop it in the microwave—and voilà! They'll never know the difference,* and a short while later, I noticed that Pippi was gone. I glanced around the room in alarm, and a moment later he emerged from the men's room with a long banner of toilet paper hanging out of the back of his pants and trailing along the floor behind him. I followed him across the room, and then I sat down next to him and told him to go back to the bathroom and clean himself up properly, didn't he see he was dragging dirty toilet paper around with him, why didn't he watch what he was doing, and why was he being so impolite, anyway, didn't he realize that I'd come all the way out here just to see him? He looked at me and seemed to remember me again all of a sudden; *Oh, Jeez, I'm sorry,* he said, and then he grew silent. I gazed around the room at the other patients sitting on plastic chairs and staring up at the television or blankly into the space before them as the crowds on the screen above danced jubilantly around the checkpoints and a few reckless spirits climbed up onto the Wall, holding their arms high in a sign of victory. Pippi resumed smoking one cigarette after the next as I watched him from the corner of my eye, this uncle I'd never met before, who had lived in a sanatorium for the past forty-five years and whom I'd never been allowed to see, whom I'd never even known about, because you never spoke of him, you never spoke much at all, and I'd dared to visit him for the first time, this man who looked more like you than all your other brothers combined. And all I knew about him was that he'd thrown Grandma's furniture out of the window one day, and that he used to take off his clothes and wander around the neighborhood until someone found him and led him back home. The afternoon passed, and at some point he asked if it would be alright if he went to lie down; it was time for his nap, he said. And when I returned to Far Rockaway a week later, he didn't know who I was anymore, and I bundled him up in his overcoat and tried to take him to the diner, but the wind was still too strong and we barely made it there when he wanted to head back, and so we returned and I sat in the lobby and watched him smoke a pack of cigarettes again, one after the next, with your eyes, your eyes fixed on the far end of the room. I finally left the sanatorium and emerged into the blinding afternoon sun, the brilliant blue sky and the wind that took my breath away, Far Rockaway, you came out here with Uncle Eddie every week, and you never said a word about it to anyone.

THE TRAFFIC ISLAND AT KOTTBUSSER TOR, where the subway stairs lead from the elevated train down to the underground line. A construction of cardboard boxes propped up against the side of the stair shaft, tied together with lengths of string. Two or three shopping carts filled with garbage bags; a sheet of plastic hanging from an opening in the cardboard wall; a few old mattresses spread out on the ground inside, covered with a thick layer of newspaper. And cars circling around ceaselessly, the traffic streaming in all directions, from Skalitzerstrasse, from Adalbertstrasse, from Reichenbergerstrasse and Kottbusserstrasse, but the island itself strangely remote, this little forgotten republic with the fenced-in stairway leading down into the ground and submerged in a sea of pigeon excrement, empty and peaceful amid the roar of cars and trucks and the subway overhead and the screaming sirens of ambulances and over and over police vans keeping tabs on the junkies across the street, and I, picturing what it's like to live there, undisturbed and for the most part forgotten in my quiet cardboard house on my own little island extending in a broad circle around me, with the rest of the world out there, beyond the distant shore.

FIDICINSTRASSE. How many times did we move the paintings, pulling them carefully out of the racks, maneuvering them around the table, the stove, tipping them forward to avoid hitting the ceiling and then turning them onto their sides, as though we were skillfully executing a sequence of precise dance steps. And careful as we were, how the corners of the paintings sometimes grazed the ceiling as we turned them around, leaving little colored lines, red, blue, turquoise, like pen marks from a compass straying off a page, parallel segments of the same broad curve. Paintings leaning up against the building in the courtyard, paintings tied up inside a rented truck, and I, gazing down the treeless street at bent figures appearing in doorways and hurrying off in the direction of the subway, listening to the sound of cars approaching over the cobblestones, resonating in the small interior of the double-parked truck and causing the tarp to beat rapidly against the truck's frame as they sped by.

How I used to imagine a gust of wind sweeping the truck up off the ground and whisking it away, me and my paintings and my jacket on the front seat with a small paper bag in the pocket, two buttered rolls with cheese and pickle, provisions for a long and uncertain journey.

FIDICINSTRASSE. Standing outside a Turkish take-out, turning over the coins in my hand and waiting for the vendor to slide open the windowpane. A small park across the street, a playground, brilliant in the afternoon sun; chestnut trees with their young, sticky buds, specks of green reflected in the storefront glass and shimmering against a web of golden branches. The shop's interior crammed full with people drinking tea, eating lunch, murky shadows barely visible behind the translucent images of swings and slides and a tilted surface rotating on a pivot like a spinning top, with children climbing onto it, trotting along it, some on wobbly legs and some dropping to their knees and spinning giddily around. A long cable strung between two posts and a seat riding swiftly along it; the dull crunching sound when the children jump off and land in the sand below. Listening to them calling, laughing, odd bits mixed together and floating along the cool breeze; gazing into the window at the reflections of their jackets and hats in the distance, red, green, yellow, illuminated against a dark background of coats pressed up to the glass in front of me, customers crowded behind the counter, waiting to pay. The sparkling of the trees, the bright sun shining on the façades of the buildings beyond, and then, from behind, two dim eyes suddenly glaring back at me, a woman inside the take-out, eyeing me through the storefront glass. And then I realize: she thinks I'm staring at her, and what do I look like to her, a figure brightly lit in a shaft of sunlight, squinting intently, unwaveringly in her direction. How should she know that I can barely see her, and that I was merely lost in thought, studying the playground over my shoulder, across the street behind me?

FIDICINSTRASSE, and the travel bag on the floor; stockings with a run up the heel and the costume I'd worn at the ceremony, full of wrinkles now and with a cheap look about the fabric I'd never noticed before. The curled-up check from the prize money, the perforated train tickets in a small pile on my desk: already on the way to Bahnhof Zoo I'd had an uneasy feeling, passing the early-morning drunks waiting around for Ullrich's to open so they could buy their schnapps; all I wanted was to turn back and go home. But I boarded my train and later that day the director met me at the station; we drove out to his home in the countryside, discussing the details of the exhibition as grazing cows sped silently by outside the car window. I was the director's personal guest, and the following days were spent unpacking crates and installing work in accordance with his schedule, drinking my coffee to the sound of the radio news at the breakfast table each morning, riding in the passenger seat on the way into town and running out of things to say. And later in the day he would take me out to lunch, to dinner, one day in this restaurant, one day in that restaurant, and each time I was about to order he would wince and say that the fish was the only thing they did well here, or the steak. One afternoon we walked to a nearby street market for lunch, and I kept straying off happily, like a dog that hadn't been let off the leash in some time; I was just about to order a lentil soup at a stand decorated with gingham bows and run by a stout woman in a gingham apron, but then I felt obliged to accept his recommendation once again and try a local specialty instead, I can't remember what it was anymore, but I can still remember the sight of the lentil soup quite clearly, with thin slices of carrot and finely diced onion. And so it was, day after day, as I installed the paintings, installed the objects, changing the positions of the upholstered vitrines countless times until

I settled on a final arrangement and placed the objects atop their velvet cushions, fruits I'd painted over in layers and layers of white oil paint that had dried, hardened, and gradually buckled inwards as the fruit shriveled underneath and all that was left was a small, wrinkled shell. And most of them were light and fragile, with a few dried-up seeds rattling around inside, the rest having dissolved to dust and the remaining oil paint skin a kind of fossil imprint of the fruit's decay. One of them was as heavy as a stone, however, a black radish that had shrunk to the size of an egg and still emitted a stench of rot that remained concealed by the vitrine's glass covering. And then the press arrived, and the director guided us to a lobby with a circle of chairs upholstered in black vinyl whose seats were so low that we all unexpectedly dropped backwards into them, all except the director, winding up in what was almost a reclining state and then grappling our way back to an upright position. I sat perched on the edge of my seat and the editor sat perched on the edge of his as the director expounded on his institution and all he'd accomplished until then, all he still intended to accomplish, the horizons that were still beckoning, the frontiers that still had to be conquered, addressing himself to the editor who had neglected to review the exhibitions of the past two years and who now, although he'd evidently found the awarding of the prize to be an event noteworthy enough to engage a photographer and make the trip from the neighboring city, was already glancing at his watch. Shouldn't we just take a walk around the exhibition, I offered, and the editor nodded his head vigorously; we struggled out of our chairs and headed for the adjoining exhibition space, abandoning the director in mid-sentence. That evening at dinner, as I sat studying the menu, wondering if I would be permitted to order on my own this time, the director confessed that he might be a little difficult to get along with these days; his lady friend had broken off with him a short time previously, he said. And every woman before her, he added, had, in fact, been unable to put up with him for long and had left her set of keys on the kitchen table one morning with a brief note tucked under the vase; the same set of extra keys passed along from hand to hand, I thought, and for the first time I found myself almost liking him, although I was caught off guard by this unexpected intimacy and having difficulty shifting into a more personal mode. And did I find him too dominant, too overbearing as well, he wanted to know. What in the world should I say, I wondered with dismay, failing to hear him properly as he smiled wistfully into his wine glass and asked if we couldn't say *Du* to one another, to change from the second person polite to the familiar. And all at once I found myself stammering *What? What?* with an almost hysterical note, because I thought he had just made another decision on what I should order for dinner, whereas I'd just realized that I did, in fact, want nothing more than a simple pizza. He repeated the question, staring down at his plate, and I said *Of course* and tried to smile, and while I gazed at the stiffly folded napkin perched upon his plate like a strange bird, I forced myself to say *Du,* and continued reminding myself to say *Du* throughout the days that followed, although I thought *Sie,* each time *Sie.* Later, when the award ceremony began, the director would take his place at the podium, put on a pair of eyeglasses, and hold his speech out at arm's length; then, he'd peer up, draw the paper close to his nose, and narrow his eyes as the audience began to chuckle. He was in his element, breaking the ice with a coy dose of self-irony; I pictured how he must do this before every speech, letting the audience in on his little joke and getting them jolly. He began relating the story of our acquaintance, which hadn't been an easy acquaintance, I soon learned, but a meaningful one rich in surprise, rich in challenge. I felt my cheeks flush and a buzzing sound nestle in my inner ear; *is he alluding to something,* I wondered in alarm, is he very, very discreetly alluding to something here? And then, all at once, I heard my name; I was being beckoned to the podium by a radiant smile, an outstretched arm, and I struggled to my feet, negotiated the distance to the front of the room in a pair of heels I was unaccustomed to wearing, and proceeded to murmur something into the microphone: a short piece I'd written during a stay in Rome, an inscription that had never been made, because its nature was essentially transitory. I considered for a moment that what I'd just said didn't really make any sense, and then I began reading my poem, startled by the sound of my amplified voice, and then, suddenly, I was finished, and I looked up at the silent audience, flustered and with nothing more to say and at a loss as to what I should do next, when the director came to my aid, his gaze both questioning and prodding; it was time for me to return to my seat, and all at once I comprehended this and retreated in haste as he pronounced my name and a list of achievements, leading the gathering in a round of obedient applause. I reached my seat as the clapping subsided and the room grew silent; the director cleared his throat and began reading the German translation. He read it much better than I had, pausing and gazing into the eyes of his listeners now and again; this man was born to stand in front of an audience, I thought, and I was not, and when he finished, his eyes remained fixed on the page a moment longer, and then he gazed up, smiled, and the room broke into enthusiastic applause. After the ceremony, standing around awkwardly in my new suit, which was a little more low-cut than I'd realized, autographing the catalogue for a line of exhibition visitors,

writing *My warmest wishes for Wolfgang,
All the best for Monika,* or later, fatigued by
the repetition, simply my signature and date,
with my lipstick tucked into the waistband of
my stockings and the prize money check curled
up in my palm, having nowhere to put it,
and so I waited until no one was looking
and slipped it into my bra, *like a prostitute,*
I thought, but what else could I do.

I LOOK INTO YOUR EYES, and for a moment I believe I can see you. I am sitting to your right, pulling a cardigan over my bare shoulders and bumping into your knee as I cross one leg over another. I apologize, and I'm embarrassed at my own clumsy apology. If only I could transform myself, turn myself into a bird at the blink of an eye, or a butterfly; I'd perch on your shoulder, I'd be a moment of delight and not this ache I am seeking to conceal. Again and again, I find myself searching for a sign, something to tell me that I am alive and not merely dreaming. If I could be the embodiment of your desire, if I could be that glass on the table before you, the one your hand is reaching for; if I could become that glass the moment you raise it to your lips to take a sip, I would do so—and I would stay here with you, in this garden, forever.

KENT AVENUE, and the day I came back from Berlin, that week I spent with you in March, how free I felt, and how relieved, wheeling my suitcases through the automatic glass doors, out of the airport, the keys to the loft in my coat pocket, the money for the taxi folded separately in my wallet. An unusually cold April, unusually wet, walking down Wythe Avenue in the rain, and dreary dreary Brooklyn all around, the ramshackle two-story houses, the junk in the yards, and new brick buildings springing up here and there, with iron fences and plush green lawns littered with debris blown, thrown over the fence, absurdly optimistic attempts at suburban transplantation. And the ragged plastic bags caught in the branches of the trees, everywhere these ragged strips of plastic flapping from naked branches. That rainy April, the translation of the book, and the memory of the week with you, that last night wrapped in the stained woolen blanket in the big room, shivering, because I couldn't bear to sleep next to you any longer.

KENT AVENUE, and all the preparation work I'd done towards getting a teaching job, all the dogged correspondence. I'd already flown to New York once that year for the interviews: staying at Joan's place; watching Star Trek on television in the evening and helping her figure out a way to get rid of a roommate who hadn't been paying his half of the rent for months. A bizarre story line involving an alien species that settles into the body at death, mingling with the memory and character of the deceased and maintaining the human shell as its home. Telltale furrows on the forehead, a greyish complexion, and the next day, walking to the West Side for an eleven o'clock appointment and stopping every ten steps or so to pull up my sock, musing over the alien that still strongly resembled the woman whose body it now inhabited, reaching into her past, drawing on her loves, her habits; was the woman still alive in some way, or was it a mere imprint of her lost self that the alien had absorbed?

I sat waiting in an air-conditioned lobby until the chairman of the department appeared in a pair of shorts, looking as though he were about to embark on his summer vacation. A vigorous shake of the hand, a terse apology, and I was escorted into another room, where I spread my transparencies over a light box and the chairman studied them with interest as dark shadows crept eerily upwards from his chin, his cheeks, and his brow. Suddenly, he straightened up with a smile. Get in touch as soon as you're back in New York; we'll schedule a lecture for the fall, and then we'll discuss the rest. And then he rushed off with my package of slides and catalogues under his arm, and all at once I had to think of how the ship's doctor had given the woman an injection to suppress her external alien attributes, the point of the plot being that she was an unusual borderline case, with a perception of self still for the most part in keeping with her former human state. And then her furrows, the grey complexion gradually disappeared and her appearance was restored to normal (as it later turned out, however, parts of her memory weren't at all complete, and an odd foreign word would slip out now and again to everyone's great consternation). That week in June, the beautiful clear weather, and then the sudden heat wave: how it felt as though my flesh were boiling beneath my skin, walking around in a daze and searching for air-conditioned bookstores to hide in until I caught a summer flu. And then I remembered that the injection was meant to be more than cosmetic; it served to arrest a slow process of transmog-rification during the course of which the alien would grow to be a distinct being as more and more of the human host's identity dissolved. The morning of the flight back to Berlin; how I waited on Joan's front steps, and how the shuttle bus never arrived and I had to drag my suitcase over to Second Avenue and hail a taxi, shivering with a fever in the ninety-eight-degree heat. The flight a mere blur; a five-hour delay in Brussels, stretched out over three seats and trying to rest. And then, in my delirium, remembering that I had to telephone you somehow and discovering that I'd lost my voice. Slipping a note across the counter to a well-groomed lady from the airline company, who dialed the number with the tip of her ballpoint pen as I stood helplessly by, surrounded by a group of furious passengers demanding information on their connecting flights and unable to utter a single word.

KENT AVENUE, and the blowups of newspaper photographs I'd papered to the walls:
five thousand square feet of digital material,
a fortune in carefully negotiated sponsorship
going to waste as I sat at my desk each day,
surrounded by Aung Sang Suu Kyi, Pinochet,
a Palestinian girl named Heuam, image en-
sembles extending from floor to ceiling and
dissolving into broad fields of enlarged dots.
The last paragraph of an article on Sarajevo
from the *New York Times Magazine*, yellowed
with age and blown up to fifty times its original
size; small-case letters as large as my hands.
*But from time to time … one thing comes into
my mind and it hurts me. I'm looking at pictures of my mom and my brother and I start
wondering, what's happening to their bodies
now, what do they look like in the ground?
And that is something that is killing me.*
Mornings spent in the 42nd Street Library
researching for the translation of a text on
ancient Egyptian embalming rites. Before the

process of desiccation could begin, each organ had to be contained separately in a Canopic jar; the remaining soft tissues and bodily fluids were dissolved in a base solution and pumped out rectally, and the brain was drawn out through the nose with a special hook. *See, you are doubly mourned. Your arms are a waterway at the fair season of inundation; your knees are enclosed with gold; your breast is a thicket of swamps; your toes guide you on fair paths; your fingers are picks of gold and their nails are knives of flint in the faces of those who would harm you.* The heart alone was wrapped carefully and placed back in its original location. A few days later, leaning across Christopher's desk and asking him if he thought that his students were looking for meaning in life, searching for it in their art, or if they mostly dreamed of becoming successful, the apparent immortality of fame. And had he told them that probably none of them ever would, or perhaps there would be one who would, one who'd shoot up like a rocket and be everywhere, his work in every museum, his face printed on the cover of every magazine, until they'd wonder at the metamorphosis in the sound of his name, an ordinary name that no longer carried an ordinary ring because it had been pronounced by too many people, had been printed too many times, because fame had turned it into a trademark, how will that be for them, I wonder. Can they imagine that, years later when the majority of them will have wound up in other professions—the one glass too many at a party, the imprudent admission: did I ever tell you I studied with *So-and-So?* The raised eyebrows; the odd juxtaposition of the extraordinary and the utterly unmemorable. Christopher led me into a cubicle where a graphic designer was working on the layout of the upcoming issue, a little laboratory where careers were concocted, names forged into currency. My eyes wandered across the wall of publications and exhibition catalogues to the window and the buildings beyond, across Broadway, where the afternoon sun was casting improbably long shadows: attenuated lines from the smallest of irregularities stretching for yards across the buildings' façades, as though the hour of hyperbole had arrived. I saw myself standing in front of a studio class lecturing to a group of students. Art is not a profession, I would tell them, *and there is nothing I can teach you.* And there they would sit, slumped in their chairs with knowing smiles, drumming their pencils idly on their knees and waiting for the quip, the punch line that wouldn't come; an uncomfortable silence would begin to grow like a big, awful balloon, steadily filling the room with its odd, tight breath and threatening to smother everything inside it. And then they'd boo me away, laugh me away, because their parents were paying a fortune to send them to art school, and they had every right to their illusions.

A CHILD SITTING ON A CARPET with a small pile of brightly colored blocks before him. His brow is set in concentration as his hand reaches for a block, deposits it into a box, and reaches for another, yet he isn't collecting them according to color, or according to size; his is a different system, one I am unable to comprehend. Sometimes his hand moves towards a certain block and hesitates, and then he reaches for another instead, and I can find nothing in the sequence of his choice to explain this correction, no particular preference for the blocks closest by, or for any particular pattern. He simply seems to notice a certain block, to see it in a way that sets it apart from every other block surrounding it, and his expression is one of firm decision as he reaches for the block, takes it into his hand, and drops it into the box as his eyes wander back to the carpet once more. One block dropped into the box, and then another, one by one each block is dropped into the box, and when he's finished, he takes them out again, one by one, flinging them onto the carpet where they were before.

KENT AVENUE, and the trees that had grown along the fences in the neighborhood, chain-link fences closing off empty lots filled with used refrigerators and rusty car parts. Weeds no one had bothered to cut back, supple shoots winding in and out between the diamond-shaped grids, weaving through like sewn threads and growing from year to year until their stalks began to stiffen into branches and there could no longer be a question of unraveling them; they were inextricable now. And then the spring came, and there was an explosion of green everywhere, the first fresh leaves sprouting from the bound trunks. And here and there a tree had been cut down, and a segment of chopped wood would remain caught in a fence, because the trunk had grown and swelled, incorporating the wire into its wounded flesh and covering it with layers of scarred bark.

KENT AVENUE, and the terrible cold I had; how it got worse each day as I sat in the dark with the slide projector, studying each image that appeared on the wall and fabricating reasons for canceling the lecture. Now and again, a tiny wisp of trembling lint became caught in one of the slide's frames, and I watched its shadow whip wildly across the projected image like a tree branch in a violent storm. Flora wrote the names of homeopathic remedies on a tea bag wrapper, Pulsatilla, Belladonna, and I finally found them at a Korean deli on First Avenue. The proprietor rang up the amount on the register, carefully concealing a hint of wry amusement as he nudged the advertising display into a more prominent position. The next day, sitting at the podium and looking out onto an audience of expectant faces and thinking for a moment that I might be dreaming; I cleared my throat and began to read, and then, all at once, the door opened and a head of orange hair appeared in a narrow shaft of light. Someone waiting to use the room; a momentary mix-up; a woman from the conference staff murmured an apology, the door closed, and I resumed reading to a hushed room as the sound of my own voice seemed to be coming from somewhere outside my own skull. How quickly I'd recognized her. The weeks that followed: how I postponed contacting the schools where I'd interviewed and continued working on the book instead, but that came later. The school year was already well under way, they were expecting my call, yet I put it off day by day until the semester drew to a close and it had already grown far too late and I had no other choice but to accept my own paralysis: six months of electronic mails, ninety-nine telephone calls, and why was I unable to make the hundredth; but that came later. The conference at the Algonquin Hotel continued for several days, and I went back to breathe in the academic air a little while longer; a young professor was lecturing on Peirce's theories. *Fallibilism: in epistemology, the view that it is not necessary for factual beliefs to be established as certain beyond the possibility of doubt.* Out of the corner of my eye, I noticed someone entering the aisle of folding chairs I was seated in; I pulled my coat onto my lap and continued listening. *Peirce's pragmatic maxim was a theory of meaning contingent on the experienceable difference between a proposition's being true and its being false, whereas James put forward a pragmatic theory of truth as something which is ultimately satisfying to believe.* I glanced sideways and saw the orange hair, the measuring blue eyes: there was an entire room full of empty seats, yet Jeanne had chosen the one next to mine as though a mysterious magnetic force were at work that kept tossing her in my direction, again and again. She leaned over and asked me the name of the professor lecturing; I told her I didn't know, lent her my program, and took the opportunity to study her more closely.

I hadn't seen her in almost twenty years; she didn't seem to remember me. She was holding the program close to her face and squinting; it was as though I had died and then slipped back in an invisible form to peer into the eyes of the living with impunity. *Peirce criticized Descartes' epistemology for its intuitionism, which holds that there are some items of absolutely certain, self-evident knowledge.* Did you know that this is almost exactly like a dream, I wanted to say, you and I, after all these years—and how is it that you don't remember me sitting in your penthouse on Sutton Place with the research I'd done for you spread out on the table between us, how is it that you don't remember me gazing up at the row of Warhols—*are they originals?*, I asked in a stammer—how is it that you don't remember the contempt in your hoarse laugh as you got up from the table to straighten the frame of one that was hanging slightly askew?

KENT AVENUE, and how I sometimes stood staring at the empty space, dreaming of building a closet to store the paintings that had been in my mother's basement in the dark all these years. But to move everything to Brooklyn on a commercial lease seemed a foolhardy thing to do, and I never built the closet, never went and got the paintings, and when the following summer arrived, I returned to Berlin and forgot about it. And then my mother sold the house; but that came later. I was still nursing the baby, and so I hired Emma to drive out to Staten Island and cart the paintings back to Brooklyn, where she sorted them out and packed them in bubble wrap and built the crates for shipping. The following weeks were riddled with ominous feelings by day and anxious dreams at night: crossing a river on a wobbly raft with all our furniture crowded around us, all our books piled up in teetering stacks, and everything tied together to forestall its toppling over from the water's rhythmic movement. And where were we going, and what is that, just a bunch of old paintings, just a bunch of old sketchbooks; don't be ridiculous. Eve and Emma on the telephone at my mother's house: we're in the basement now, there's an old bureau here, an old trunk, and I at the other end of a six-hour time difference, with my throat too dry to speak. Eve's pragmatic manner: what should we junk, what about this old mirror, what about the rocking chair? Sitting at my desk with my eyes closed and my ear pressed to the phone, trying to picture them standing there, actually standing there in the basement, two emissaries sent into my past, like astronauts in the outer space of my imagination, their heads nearly grazing the low stucco ceiling, the two reliefs of deer in the woods my mother once made in ceramics class on the wall at the foot of the stairs and Grossmutter's dresser with the curved legs that I used to trace my fingers along when I was still small enough to crawl underneath it. Emma reading out the inventory over the telephone: an old fur coat, a tin cake box with a picture of Manhattan on the lid, a pair of ice skates, a chess set. The sound of her voice reading out the titles of the books, Dostoyevsky, Joyce, and a few old school books, *Leggendo e Ripassando, Le Avventure di Giovanni Passaguai*. A staple gun, paintbrushes, do you want this? No, throw it away. Emma's descriptions: I have an object here that's made of bronze, a small fat man in a turban; his face is contorted in a grimace and his head opens on a hinge. And I: send that, oh send that, a souvenir you'd picked up in a port during the war; how can she know what it means to me? Send it, throw it away, send it, throw it away. Emma's voice a medium conjuring images from the distant past, and I at the other end, trying to stem my anxiety, trying to conceal my desperation; just a few personal things, just a shipping problem. The sketchbooks, the paintings, and a terrible feeling of something being there that I didn't want anyone to see, something terribly private, and all of it packed into overseas crates, stored now somewhere in a warehouse in Brooklyn and waiting to be hauled onto the container of a freight ship. Holding a slip of paper in my hands with the date of departure, the name of the ship printed on it: my paintings, my youth will sink on the Madison Maersk somewhere between New York and Hamburg, originally scheduled to arrive on April 13.

THE SUDDEN SQUAWK OF A BLACKBIRD on the roof of the building across the street; how I went over to the window and watched it, watched it pick at something and then stop and squawk. And how it began picking at this thing again, picking at it and dragging it a few feet across the roof with its beak, and how it stopped and squawked again, squawking and picking at it and dragging it a little further, and then I saw that the thing it was dragging was a dead bird, another blackbird. And how it finally abandoned the dead bird and flew up onto the water tower, crying out again and again before finally flying away.

FIDICINSTRASSE, and the day we finally decided to throw some of the junk away, the layers of rugs Christoph had dragged in from the street to insulate the cold floor, the lengths of battered oven pipe. How we finally transported a truckload to the city refuse facility, where we watched long lines of discarded goods progress down a conveyor belt before dropping into the open fire of the incinerator below. Unwanted furniture, blankets, broken appliances, haphazardly united this one time, on this one last journey, illuminated in a hellish glow. We stood watching the wide belt carry its unending procession, objects of all types and sizes one by one tipping over the edge and falling into the fiery pit. And then my eyes fell upon a photograph of a man in a gilt frame, and I fought an urge to run after it, retrieve it, this portrait of a man peering out from a world long since gone. And the last living person who'd known him having recently died, perhaps: an old woman whose furniture had been sold off, whose name had been removed from the doorbell, whose apartment had been cleared out for new tenants to move in, the floors sanded, the walls painted, a photograph that hadn't been seen by anyone else for years. And now, the man's eyes looking into my own, and I the last person to witness this testimony of his existence, *but who were you,* I wanted to cry out as I watched the photograph approach the edge of the belt, darken in silhouette against the bright orange background, and disappear. I look at the photographs on my own desk, at the objects arranged in a particular order, surrounding me, reflecting my thoughts back to me; objects even the most banal of which will survive me, pass on to other hands, enter other orders. And the secrets they contain will have been silenced, but perhaps they will continue to exist somewhere within, who knows. The arrangements I made when I was a child, when I went to play in a small schoolyard on

Guyon Avenue: rows of pine cones and acorns and other things I'd found on the ground, a book of matches, a piece of tin foil, the heel of a ladies' shoe. What was in those arrangements, was it the unknown histories these objects possessed, was it the fascination for a school I didn't attend, filled with children I'd never met, a parallel world in which everything was similar, yet different: the monkey bars in the playground, the cement turtles, a semicircle of steps leading down into a paved arena in the manner of a small coliseum. How we went there after school to play, after all the children had gone home; how I rode my bicycle down the cement steps, *bump bump bump,* and how the schoolyard seemed to belong so much more to me than to anyone else. And we would balance on the top rungs of the monkey bars with our feet hooked under the bar below, crisscrossing our arms against our chests and clapping our hands once on our knees, once in front, and then slapping them three times together to the rhythm of the words we sang, *Miss Mary Mac, Mac, Mac, all dressed in black, black, black, with silver buttons, buttons, buttons, all down her back, back, back.*

FIDICINSTRASSE, and the smell of smoke
coming from next door; I hurried out into the
hallway and sniffed at Frau Chran's door, and
then I began to knock, calling out *Frau Chran,
Frau Chran!* as I stared at the sign above the
doorbell with her name written in a shaky
hand. I stopped and listened intently, but could
hear nothing, and then I began knocking more
loudly until I was finally pounding on the door,
kicking it with my shoe, and all at once I heard
Frau Chran's voice from behind and the sound
of her fumbling with a set of keys and turning
the lock. And then the door opened a crack,
and I pushed against it, only to discover that
the chain was still attached, and all of a sudden
I was furious. *Let me in! Something's on fire!* and
Frau Chran, with a look of fear and confusion
in her eyes, too flustered to speak, obeyed and
slid back the chain. I hurried past her into
the hallway, which was already filling up with
smoke, past the coats and umbrellas and into
the living room, where a Christmas decoration

hanging above a sideboard had caught fire, one long burning garland strung across the wall, and beneath it a smoking candle with a little ruffle of holly buried under mounds of blackened wax. I ran into the kitchen and finally found a bucket under the sink crammed full of flower pots and withered bulbs; I turned the knob of the faucet as far as it would go, but nothing more than a thin stream of water trickled out. Frau Chran came into the kitchen, *you shouldn't be using that bucket,* she began, *I have another one right here somewhere,* and she began poking around in the corner with her cane; I scolded her for not alarming me sooner, and she peered around at me in terror, and then I wondered for the first time if her mind wasn't going: she'd been acting strangely lately, hadn't she, and hadn't we found her out in the courtyard in her slippers a few times, squinting around in confusion, and led her gently back inside. *I have to call the fire department,* I thought frantically, but then I remembered

that Frau Chran had had her number discon-
nected several months previously to save the
expense, and I realized that I would have to get
her out of the apartment somehow, that I would
have to make the call next door, and all at once
Frau Chran began to whimper. Frau Chran,
we have to leave, we have to call for help, I said
as I tried to guide her out of the kitchen, but
she pushed my hand away and cried out *What?
What are you saying?* And I shouted *We have
to leave!* and yanked her by the elbow, but she
struck out with her cane and lost her balance
and nearly fell to the floor and I caught her just
in time. *I'm not leaving, I'm not leaving,* she
screamed, her hands clasped around my arms,
and then I saw that the bucket was nearly full,
and I freed myself from her grip and sat her
down on a chair and pulled the bucket out of
the sink, ran into the living room with water
splashing out along the way, and threw the bucket onto the flaming garland as a loud hiss rose
up in the room. I opened the window and sat

down on the edge of the couch to view the wet and smoldering mess. The wallpaper was singed with long, black streaks that grazed the ceiling; a layer of oily soot had settled on the room like a sticky veil. Frau Chran came hobbling into the living room; she was wailing now, *you won't tell anyone, will you?* and for the first time I understood that she was afraid of being taken away against her will, put in a home. She'd been doing her own shopping and carrying her own coal up from the basement for years, and then Angelika started giving her a hand, but she still did her own cooking, and she'd never dream of giving anyone a spare key; Frau Chran was mistrustful of everyone. *I have a little savings,* she began, and a crafty expression crept over her face, *if you could find me a nice young man who'll paper the room,* and then I heard myself telling her that everything would be alright, *we'll get this mess cleaned up and a fresh coat of paint on the walls and no one will ever know what happened,* but I knew it was only a matter of time until someone would find out, assess the danger she was beginning to present to the rest of the building's inhabitants, and notify the authorities.

FIDICINSTRASSE. The tea balls drying on a bed of tea leaves in a shoe box cover balanced on top of the radiator in the kitchen: how it dried out from the heat as well, the glue-drenched tea contracting and the rectangular form of the box contorting until the corners curled up like a little boat. And the balls themselves, one each day, left over from the morning tea and pressed into tight spheres by the sieve; I arranged them into little piles on the windowsill after they'd dried. Beneath it, the enamel paint buckling out from the damp and crumbling off the wall, and over the black spots of fungus forming underneath, entire areas that were still intact: thin, brittle, bubbly sheets of paint attached here and there at a few fragile points. And I was always afraid to touch it, afraid the whole thing would disintegrate. The pattern of erosion on the floor in the kitchen: how first the white of the seal became visible from underneath the enamel paint, here and there along the cracks between the panels of pressed wood, around

the sunken screws, and then the naked board itself wore through, each year a little more. And
how the pressed wood swelled with moisture
each time we mopped the floor; how the moisture crept and caused the floor paint to wrinkle,
here and there, a little bit of paint chipping off
each time. How many hundreds of evenings did
I gaze at the floor, gaze at the pattern, looking
for a form to pour my thoughts into, tracing
them in the wandering edge of the curling paint.
Searching for something to say, searching for
the words to break your silence.

WHEN DOES A PLACE CEASE TO BE A PLACE, when does a person become a location? Flora told me that after her father had died, her mother moved out of the house she'd grown up in, at first to her parents' home, and later to an apartment in the center of town. And some years later she moved again, and the new apartment was a little smaller than the previous one, and then she moved once more, and each time she moved, the apartments grew smaller and smaller. And whenever Flora came back to visit, she would search in vain for some certain thing she remembered from long ago, and her mother, having less and less room to put things, wouldn't be able to reconstruct where it could be—*is it in your grandparents' basement, is it at So-and-So's?*—unable, perhaps, to admit that she'd discarded anything along the way at all, until there was eventually nothing left that could remind Flora of home, only, perhaps, her mother's body.

ALL THAT'S LEFT OF NINTH STREET: three crates in Freihafen Hamburg, 2,100 pounds balanced on a forklift driven by a dock worker so skillful in the handling of his machine that its movements seemed as discreet as the gentle nudge of a gloved hand. Two long, flat prongs prodding the crates as he helped us load the truck: a little bit to the left, a little bit forward, maneuvering them easily, dexterously, plywood crates that were impossible for a human to lift, to even budge. The hours spent waiting at customs, the queue of disgruntled truck drivers leaning against a wall and gazing now and again at a red light blinking weakly above a steel door, waiting for it to turn green and summon the next in line. How a uniformed official would occasionally emerge with a clipboard under his arm, as often as not followed by a driver ordered to open his truck for inspection as the others in line chuckled quietly. And later, the drive back to Berlin; a storm beating up against the windshield, the wind and the weight slowing the truck down considerably. And what if we never arrive? Once, long ago now, I crept down the basement stairs and began opening and closing boxes, taking things out and unwrapping them, rewrapping them, why, I don't know, I was trying to find an order I could reconcile myself to, perhaps, trying to find a form I could better commit to memory. And days later, in a sudden fit, unwrapping everything once more because something didn't feel quite right, something felt awful, and I spent days searching for another order: packing, unpacking, repacking boxes, again and again, this book, this artifact from my past, what to keep, what to throw out, these crates in the back of the truck, full of paintings and cardboard boxes filled with God knows what and still arranged in the final, unsatisfactory order I'd left them in years ago, when I began avoiding the basement any time I visited the old house. It was dark when we finally arrived, lowered the lifting platform, and rolled the crates into the building on the jacklift. And then we stood there at a loss, because one of them was an inch too wide, another an inch too high for the elevator, and so we unloaded them in the hallway and drove home. (Days later, after unscrewing the plywood covers and gathering the Styrofoam packing material into plastic bags, when the paintings were leaning against the wall and there was only one canvas left in the largest crate—how you motioned for me to come and feel the cool air trapped behind it, how it lightly blew across my cheek as we pulled the painting out, this air still chilled from the journey overseas, from the cold rainy days stored in Hamburg's harbor). And later, my studio filled with paintings wrapped in bubble plastic, paintings I recognized immediately, but somehow remembered differently; paintings I'd entirely forgotten, that I was as embarrassed to see as if they'd been photographs of my adolescent self in a variety of awkward hairstyles, hidden away in my mother's basement and tying me to the house for years.

NINTH STREET, and the day you packed my things into boxes before leaving the apartment for good. And now, seventeen years later, or rather yesterday, seventeen years to the day, but I didn't see that, didn't realize that last night as I sat cross-legged on the floor of my room and slowly, reluctantly began to unwrap. A small cardboard box with blue printed letters on four sides: BON TON CORN CHIPS, 25¢, REGULAR, BAR-B-QUE; the little square next to REGULAR is marked with an X. Your handwriting on the top flap in magic marker: CONTENTS: BUREAU STUFF, written in green; FRAGILE, written in red. Unfolding the brittle newspaper, the smell of mildew hanging in the air like a quiet threat; pages from the Business Day section of the *New York Times*. CAREER MARKETPLACE, BUSINESS DIGEST, REAL ESTATE MART, N.Y.S.E. BONDS. *"Unocal Offers 28.8% Stock Buyback for $72 Debt"; "Coca-Cola Changing Formula."* I looked at the date: April 24, 1985. I must have repacked some of the things in fresh newspaper after emptying the apartment on Ninth Street and driving everything out to Staten Island. But no, I thought as I woke up this morning, that can't be—and I suddenly remembered that I hadn't returned to New York until the following year and that you'd already moved out of the apartment six months after I left for Berlin and sublet the place to someone named Andy who played the didgeridoo. The newspapers were from the day you packed my things away for storage; some time passed before I realized that yesterday's date had been the twenty-fourth of April. And hidden away inside the yellowed pages: Grandma's carved wooden jewelry box with the mirror and the yellow brocade lining stretching smoothly over the hinge, holding the cover in place when the box was open; how I left it outside to air out, peering through the glass of the balcony door at my own reflection inside the box, and how the fabric suddenly tore from age. And the photographs: Grandma in a wedding dress, a broad white hat and elegant shoes, holding a huge bouquet of white flowers; the passe-partout is embossed with the photographer's imprint: J. J. GOODMAN, 149TH STR. & 3RD AVE. Slowly, slowly; not too much at once. In another cardboard box, beneath your Blue-jacket's Manual, the Coast Guard beret you once wore, pressed flat now after so many years. I picked it up and felt around the crown of the hat, and my fingers happened upon something stiff, a flap in the rim and something tucked inside; I pushed it through and a book of matches fell out into my hand: Florsheim Shoes. Smoking on guard duty, the tiny orange dot in the night: a dead giveaway in the viewfinder of enemy binoculars. Later, I would lower the beret carefully into a bucket of soapy water, rinse it out, and fit it over the rim of a wide bowl, leaving it outside to dry. But the odor of mildew wouldn't leave, not entirely, and so I left it on the balcony in the sun and checked it each morning to see if the smell was gone yet, as though I were waiting for a ghost to finally depart. Going through another one of the wooden boxes, postcards of paintings and prints from The National Gallery, The Victoria and Albert Museum, The Rijksmuseum; a photograph of Virginia Woolf, the death mask of William Blake, and an odd thing here and there in between: an X-ray of a tooth in a small manila envelope with the names *Chin, Frank, Dr. Yamada,* and the date, *5/24/44,* written with a fountain pen in fine script; an international driving permit issued on April 3, 1974 by the Kanagawa Prefectural Public Safety Commission to Takaaki Nagashima, born April 1, 1943 in Tokyo and residing at 28-30 Mitsuzawa-Shimo-Cho, Kanagawa-Ku, Yokohama; a slip of paper I must have found in the street one day, a list of things to do for someone named Rob: *1. Laff. Lofts needs a pick-up in the morning, the ¾ yd. cont. outside; 2. Jack Schwartz Shoe Store at 138 Duane Street has about 6 to 8 boxes outside tonight—don't leave it out* (underlined twice); 3. *Did you give the sticker to the Plymouth store* ... followed by an arrow, and, on the reverse side of the slip: *at 111 John Street yesterday* (also underlined twice): a vague feeling of recognition, but what, what, and an old postcard from Berlin: *Ich liebe Dich bis in alle Ewigkeit* spray-painted on a brick wall, with the naked branches of a tree just visible beyond it and a broad field of cobblestones comprising the bottom half of the photograph, dropping away in sharp perspective. I turned the card around and was surprised to see my own handwriting, an older handwriting, the handwriting of a woman I'd long since ceased to be: *I'll translate this for you when I come home,* the card addressed to you, the stamps postmarked; you must have slipped it in among my papers while you were packing my things. *I love you to all eternity:* a sullen reproach that I would discover seventeen years later, seventeen years to the day.

THE SMELL OF NINTH STREET, but no, the things didn't smell of mildew back then, all the little wooden boxes I collected, the straw suitcase, the newspaper wasn't yellowed back then, it's not the smell of Ninth Street pervading my room now, but the smell of organisms that bred in the dark, damp basement on Staten Island. Rubbing the wooden boxes with furniture oil, leaving them open on the balcony to air out, is there any way to get rid of this odor pervading the books, the papers, Grandma's cotton doilies, nauseating me. I open the window up wide and let in the cool night air; a thick folder of papers is sitting on the desk before me. College essays on Fouquet, on Plato, on Sartre. A treatment of Hans Haacke's socio-political installation on the unsavory facts behind Mobil Oil's patronage of the arts. *Life in the present is a somewhat shapeless conglomerate of possible apparitions ... Antoine realizes that every time he recalls a precious memory, he risks the danger of los-*

ing it to words, which will then replace the image, replace the sensation in the memory. The telephone rings; it's Anselm. Last-minute corrections; the publication has to be at the printer's in the morning. Were you sleeping? No, I tell him, I was only reading; I've got the file in front of me now. *Weltanschauung,* he begins. *Commercially fictionalized iconography.* I struggle to concentrate; among the papers on the desk before me is a photograph of my studio taken twenty years ago. I recognize everything; a mere blob in the grainy film suffices, and my memory reconstructs everything. I hear the sound of voices in the background, hear the sharp gasp of Anselm inhaling a cigarette. *The location of truth in the realm of Reason and Idea creates a problem in that all thought is rooted in the body ... it is illogical to postulate a truth outside of material existence, since we are at all times conceiving of it through the means of our own material existence.* The coat draped over a chair, the paintings hanging closely together on the wall. Anselm wants to know if it's okay to transpose the clauses of a particular sentence; he'd like to begin the paragraph with another image. Can't we switch it around? *Blake's objection to Reynolds' theories suggest that Blake found Reynolds' ideal of formalism an empty, if exquisitely constructed shell.* I consider telling Anselm that I'm in a very peculiar state of mind. My room reeks of the past; this very moment, just as we're speaking, the past is creeping out of every corner, did you know that? Thick wafts of past are hanging heavily in the air. Anselm's voice suddenly sounds mangled; the battery on his cell phone is running out. Then I hear nothing, and I hang up the telephone. A moment later, it rings again. Another sharp draw on the cigarette; Anselm doesn't even say hello this time. Perhaps it wouldn't be so difficult if it weren't for the smell. I prefer my reconstructions, Anselm, did you know that? It's easier to live with them than these damp, rank things. We continue going through the text; I mark each change with a yellow highlight. What was the real smell of things: the heavy aroma of oil paint, for instance, of rabbit-skin glue; the sweet scent of wood cut to build stretchers. And again and again, a cup of coffee, a lit cigarette: smells steeped in the present. *Dostoyevsky repeatedly complained that while he was involved with a "realism of a higher sense" in which truths were expressed through the patterns of human relationships, there was still something which was probably the very core of his ideas, which he would go to his grave with, without ever having communicated it to a soul.*

I saw a film once in which a dam was about to be opened and a river rerouted. An entire village was on the brink of being flooded; the authorities had long since evacuated its inhabitants. Only an old woman had stayed behind, scrubbing her hut on her bare knees, in her bare feet, scrubbing the floorboards until the grain of the wood shined through, cleaning the bed linens and the windowpanes, and then, when the house was as fresh and as rosy-cheeked as a young bride, scattering flower petals over the sparkling floorboards—one last gesture of love for a house, a past destined to disappear. And now, wouldn't I like to do the same, now that the paintings are all in one place, all the paintings from Eisenbahnstrasse, all the paintings from Fidicinstrasse, from Ninth Street—everything united for the first time in one location. And into this perfect order I'd like to throw a lit match, watch it all go up in flames, gathered together in one bright flash, forever, and there would be nothing, nothing that could disturb this order ever again.

WHY IS IT SO HARD for children to imagine their parents young, marrying and starting a family and finding it all much more difficult than they'd ever expected; finding that time passes more quickly than they'd ever expected. And one day you understood that you'd given up your dreams for good, the trail of breadcrumbs having led nowhere, and yet you dragged yourself out of bed each morning, fell back into it again each night, a temporary escape, a little death. And where was I, I was no consolation, just another mouth to feed, nothing more. I have a photograph of the graduating class of Samuel Gompers Vocational High School in the Bronx, June 1939; Class 8C Electric. Germany is very far away, Poland is very far away. A quarter of the twenty-two graduating seniors appear to be of Italian descent, a quarter Irish, another quarter Jewish. You're sitting in the front row with a broad grin and your shirt collar open wide; most of the other boys are wearing ties tucked neatly into their suits. Spread out on the desk before me are two mimeographed newsletters, *The Gompers Voice* from April and June 1938. A letter from the principal, Mr. Pickett: *"When fellows are at the 'teen' age, some of them are apt to consider that baseball and football are ... perhaps the most important things in life. However, as boys grow older, this viewpoint changes. It is well, therefore, to endeavor to acquire, even when one is young, some idea of relative value."* And on the back, an ink drawing of a balled-up hand, and then another, better drawn and more resolute; "SCRIMA'S FIST" is printed alongside it, with an arrow pointing at the hand. Above them are the drawn profiles of several figures whose noses have apparently been punched in; one of them is labeled "RUBY": BEFORE, with a hook nose, and AFTER, the nose flattened, the eyes widened in a woeful expression. *Nobody likes a sissy. It can be safely said that Gompers boys are not sissies ...* Other sketches made in pen:

a Chinaman in a silk robe and pigtail, then with a Western haircut and suit; you hadn't yet turned seventeen. *Don't Forget Your Lunch! Gompers Field Day, June 9 at Pelham Bay Park … Many of us know and many of us do not know that the man after whom our school is named was a son of a London cigar maker.* On the following page, a pupil's report about a *New York Times* article on the first graduating class of the modern industrial high school, followed by a poem: *Great leader of labor, defender of right, / Often they've cheered your wisdom and might; / Men say you have died, but your name is immortal / Preserved for eternity on our school's portal …* Next to it is an article about a school play on urban poverty, describing the stage set, an exact replica of a four-story slum tenement in flowery euphemisms; was the building you grew up in all that different, I wonder. One of your sketchbooks contains a sepia drawing of a view into a run-down court-yard: a worn brick façade, battered tin pipes on the roof, lines of washing extending from fire escapes. A few more drawings from the time: Mr. Schur, English Teacher; Clark Gable; Theodore Roosevelt. Another drawing of a woman smiling, with brown marks of cellophane tape staining the edge of the lined paper; 11–18–43 is written underneath, a little over a month before your twenty-second birthday. And next to it—how is it I've never seen it before—written in pencil and then erased: MY WIFE. I stop and stare at the page; the baby is crawling around beneath my feet. Suddenly, he pulls the plug out of the wall and the computer goes dead: everything I've been writing is lost, I will have to write everything again, everything I know about Gompers High, but here it is, the first time I'm seeing a picture of your first wife, Wanda, and then it occurs to me that a whole set of pictures once existed, pictures I've never seen, pictures of you and Wanda, wedding photographs, picnics, a part of your life we never knew anything about. Is Wanda still alive, I wonder, and was it a cruel irony, years later, when you moved into the new house with a new wife and three kids and not a single tooth left in your head to find yourself living next door to not one Wanda, but two?

OLD WORK IN BUBBLE FOIL stacked against the walls of my studio; seven large garbage bags filled with Styrofoam balls. Grossmutter's trunk, a relic from the emigration, back in Germany again after seventy-seven years in the Bronx, after forty years on Staten Island, propped open in one corner of the studio now, the sketchbooks and journals inside airing out. When I was a child, lifting the heavy lid was like crossing the border to another country, filled with old woolen blankets and mothballs that shrank over time as the camphor evaporated, little white crystalline balls of varying size, some of which were no bigger than dots. The brittle paper lining the trunk, printed in stripes that had once been white and pale ochre in color; the leather handles that had long since broken off. I bend over the trunk and open one of the journals warily: a description of an old dream. I close it and return it to its former place. Later, unable to resist, I will unpack everything and arrange it on top of the flat files: the old plastic stagecoach, the little bronze man whose head opens on a hinge, an ancient cowbell, an ornate silver ladle. And what was in the trunk a hundred and seventeen years ago, I wonder, and has anything made this journey twice: Grossmutter's salt and pepper shakers, for instance, Grossvater's tin coffee pot, forgotten at the back of a kitchen cupboard until I wrapped it in newspaper and stashed it away with the other things in the basement twenty-odd years ago. Packed into a brand-new traveling trunk and locked with a shiny key, a key long since lost, departing from the very same dock, perhaps, that it would return to a hundred and seventeen years later; it's not impossible. And where does this all take me, where does this thinking take me? All these things, fascinating me, suffocating me. I am hard put to throw any of them away; they possess a new kind of nobility, they have the air of world travelers now, and it's too late, I'm stuck with them for good.

AND A FEW OF YOUR SKETCHBOOKS, a few photographs, a talent test from the "Famous Artists School" in Westport, Connecticut—PRICE ONE DOLLAR, with the word FREE printed over it at an oblique angle. The notes you made on the cover: CLIPPED COUPON 4/22/55 → DOCTOR'S OFFICE WHEN NO ONE WAS LOOKING (← DR. PORITZ WON'T MIND). RECEIVED TEST 5/2/55. MAILED TEST 5/2/55. INTERVIEW (HARRY BARCLAY) 5/6/55 (P.S. GAVE $25. DEPOSIT—DENTIST CAN WAIT (← DR. BERMANN WON'T MIND). Stamped in blue beneath the cover illustration of an artist painting from a model are the words: *Based on the evidence submitted in this talent test, the admissions committee makes the following recommendations. You DO qualify for admission to the Famous Artists Schools.* The word Do is filled in with red pencil, a word you apparently pinned all your hopes on. And the next page: TELL US ABOUT YOURSELF. HOW LONG HAVE YOU BEEN INTERESTED IN

Art? *(All my life)* What museums have you visited? *(Metropolitan, N.Y.C.)* Do you have confidence in your ability to concentrate? *(Yes)* Can you follow instructions? *(Yes)* Are you willing to accept sincere criticism? *(Yes)* And on the following pages, drawing exercises: Your sense of form, your sense of observation, your imagination and originality. Other papers: a Famous Artists Dictionary; a leaflet appealing to the student to recruit new members (Portable Fold-Away All-Purpose Easel, $15.70 Value— Yours without charge when only one friend enrolls) and four postage-paid post-cards to this purpose; mailing instructions for sending in the assignments; a checklist of artist's materials from Famous Artists Materials, Inc., a subsidiary of the mail-order school, including one receipt for a wooden table easel ($2.00) and another totaling $12.10 for 24 Bainbridge illustration boards and ½ pint Artone Ink—

Extra Dense Black. There's another letter in the folder, this one from the Metropolitan Life Insurance Company at One Madison Avenue, dated December 2, 1955. *"Dear Mr. Scrima: This note is to tell you how much my associates and I enjoyed meeting with you recently ..."* The president's signature, Mr. Frederic W. Ecker, is printed in blue offset ink, presumably in an effort to simulate ballpoint pen. How long did you keep it up, I wonder, selling insurance by day and working on your commercial art assignments at night; when did you finally let go of the dream you only began pursuing at the age of thirty-four? The drawings you made of your buddies in the Coast Guard: Bill Gurrini, James O'Loughlin; the cartoons from the war (WRITING HOME: *"Dear Mazie, working us like dogs, don't get a minute's rest, etc."* ... *"Hello Joe, boy what a racket, don't do nothing, etc."*). And then, a sheet of paper with the letterhead of the school I began studying painting at many, many years later. There's a sketch of a floor plan on it; I can no longer recall who drew it, or why. It looks like a tenement apartment, perhaps our apartment on Ninth Street, but it appears to be furnished differently. You and I never spoke about art. There's a meandering line beneath it, a sloppy string of m's. We never once spoke about art, did we? I stare at the floor plan, growing uneasy. Did it hurt you, I wonder, when I set out to do the very thing you failed at? I hold the sheet of paper up to the light; I have a vague feeling of recognition, a feeling of something unpleasant, something painful, yet my memory fails me. Why did I save it, and what is it doing in the folder with your drawings?

MY MIND SNAPPED SHUT LIKE A BOX. I turn, perplexed: but wasn't something there a moment ago? Waiting, waiting, looking on as though at a mute child, hoping to pry out a word, or a smile: patience is the essence. The child stands dumbly before me, and I kneel down with a friendly mien. What was that just now, what do you have in your hand, I ask gently. The child's eyelashes veil its downcast eyes. I saw you putting something in your pocket a moment ago, wouldn't you like to show me what you have in your pocket? But the child stares at its toes, suspended in a glistening bubble of impunity. Say something, I blurt out, growing agitated, and the child raises a grimy fist to brush the hair out of its eyes, gazing at me in sullen apathy. I hear the sharp edge in my voice, I know this tactic will lead me nowhere, yet I'm vexed, I want to drill the child with questions: what are you hiding, what have you stolen? And hardly an answer, a feeble shrug, and I, growing desperate,

give it back, give it back, feeling the hand
itching to slap the face of this stupid, torpid
mind: will you come to your senses, will you
give me back what's mine?

EISENBAHNSTRASSE, and the wide arc dug into the grey linoleum floor by the door; how bright and clean it was in the huge expanse of dirty grey extending from one end of the loft to the other, like the clear track of a windshield wiper on dirty glass. The broad dip in the middle of the floor that sagged so badly that it was nearly impossible to build a stretcher in square; how the tiny red ball I threw for the cat used to bounce around, hitting a painting now and then and leaving a trail of little colored dots. The ball would bounce and bounce and then circle around the room, and the cat used to stare at the ball in transfixed attention as it rolled around and around, and in the end, when it had slowly rolled for what seemed to be the last time down into the dip in the floor, the momentum of its own weight would transport it some distance beyond the point of standstill, until, poised on the edge of the dip's incline and under the cat's watchful eye, the pull of gravity would induce it to roll back to the center of the room again, the floor's concave depression providing the ideal conditions for a perpetuum mobile. And the cat, unable to stand the suspense any longer, would as often as not pounce on it, sending it bouncing off in all directions once more. And the star spray-painted in one corner of the studio, left behind by the hippies who'd lived there before me: how it was hidden for some time by the canvases leaning up against the wall, and how, when I built the racks and moved the paintings to the other corner, it became visible all of a sudden, this lopsided star in red and black spray paint that my eyes were drawn to again and again until I finally found a silkscreen ink that created a permanent bond with the linoleum, taped out a large square, and mixed a shade of paint to cover it. And the star, extinguished now in a field of grey, but not entirely, its faintly plastic contours visible when the light from the window cast them into relief. Sometimes, when I couldn't bear to stay in the studio any longer, I went for a walk past the church and the elevated train and down to the canal, where I'd walk along the muddy path to the bridge and cross over to the opposite bank, the same walk each time, the same thoughts each time, or nearly, watching the swans drift along the littered surface of the water, snapping at a piece of stale bread now and again. On some days, the booths of the Turkish market flanked both sides of the street all the way to Kottbusserbrücke, with produce and spices and bolts of cloth spread out on large folding tables and tarps draped over a loose construction of wooden beams to keep out the rain. And crowds of people pushing past with their shopping carts and bicycles and baby carriages, squeezing through the narrow path beneath two long garlands of electric light bulbs strung up above. Sometimes I'd stop for a coffee on the corner and watch the gulls sitting on a roof on the north side of the canal, identical shapes lined up in an undeviating column and precisely equidistant, each bird separated from the next by a single wing span. One of them would pick up now and again and drift along a light current of wind, over the used cars parked along the bridge, over the heads of the men who stopped to look at them, inspecting the signs taped to the inside of their windows and comparing prices and mileage. Today, the same light wind was blowing across the plastic tablecloth before me and eddying around it somehow, causing an edge to flap rapidly against a rusty metal leg; the sun, shining upon the table's surface, blinding me with its litany of *here, now.* And suddenly, at some secret signal, the pigeons took wing and flew in one broad curve around the barges and over the bridge, and the sun, lower on the horizon now, hit upon the underside of their wings at one particular angle, one moment in which the rays of the late afternoon sunlight flickered in hundreds of wings, infusing them with a bright orange.

EISENBAHNSTRASSE, and the old portable typewriter I bought at the flea market;
the ridiculous amount of money I spent on re-
pairing the little mechanism that transports
the ribbon wheel. I carried it home and rubbed
off the fingerprints with a tissue until its black
enamel surface shined flawlessly, and then I
placed it at the center of my desk and dreamed
of writing my first book and instead began
writing letters to you, pages and pages of letters,
inserting the paper carefully into the machine
and afterwards stowing the copies away in a
folder with the sheets of used carbon paper,
tissue-thin and covered in a fragile web of overlapping sentences. And some time later, when
was that, I reread them and tore them up into
little bits and then paced around the studio
until I finally stuffed them into an empty flow-
erpot on the fire escape, poured kerosene over
it all, and lit a match. And afterwards, when
I came home, the studio was full of smoke and
the scraps of paper merely singed on the edges,

but legible, legible. And then the telephone rang, and I ran to pick it up and heard your voice for the first time again after how long, wanting to meet again, after all this time. I consented, coughing from the smoke, and then I thought the better of it and declined, laying the receiver slowly back onto the hook. And later, perhaps I passed by you on a busy street one day, not having thought of you for quite some time, not suspecting a thing: it's happened so many times before, but the other way around. A face flits by, a moment's hesitation:: *Did he see me?* You, and you. Another time, years before, I was buying a pack of cigarettes in a drugstore on First Avenue, thinking about whether I should call you this time, thinking about whether I should call anyone at all this time, when I suddenly saw you hurrying by the store front window. How I waited for my change and then ran out of the store and down the street after you, but you were so fast, you were always so fast with your nervous energy, your long, smooth stride. By the time I finally caught up, I was completely out of breath, and instead of calling out your name, I grabbed hold of your coat sleeve, gasping. How you reeled around in alarm as I stood in the middle of the street, gesticulating; how I struggled for air as I tried to explain that, had I turned my head to look out the drugstore window only a moment later, we would never have known how close our paths had come to crossing.

EISENBAHNSTRASSE, and how I'd been there once before, when was that, years before at someone's party, the unfamiliar street, the unfamiliar courtyard, the electronics factory out back and the yellow brick smokestack, a relic from a former century. And who was at the party, I can hardly remember, artists, art students, the usual scene. How I stood, drink in hand, across the hall from my future home, not imagining that my life would one day begin to imbed itself into these surroundings, that this unfamiliar street, this unfamiliar court-yard would increasingly come to contain me—until the sight of the graffiti scrawled on the wall of the building across the street upon opening the front door, or the row of mailboxes in the hallway with mine among them would become as intimate and personal as a wry smile or the flicker in someone's eye, meant for me and me alone. And then, the sight of the cat running through the courtyard and jumping onto the back of the truck in one long leap before we moved away; I'd been looking for him for hours, calling him as we carried each painting down the stairs and onto the truck, but that came later. The last of the furniture and boxes were stacked securely and the paintings tied with thick rope to the truck's frame when we gave up the search in favor of coming back later and Ernest turned the key in the ignition. How you nearly made me stop sweeping the empty loft, but I insisted, wanting one last moment alone with the space. What is that, that feeling for a room, a location, why do I still slow my pace when I pass the door to the ground-floor flat on Ninth Street on my way upstairs to Laura's? Why do I check each time to see if the light is burning behind the peephole? And each time I'll think of the spot in front of the radiator where the floorboards were so warped from the escaping steam that I always imagined a tree was struggling to push its way through, or a trapped soul, or I'll think about how my old kitchen table is probably still inside, on the other side of this heavy door with the mezuzah screwed in diagonally at the top of the frame and buried under decades of hall paint and the little round hole the dealers used to slip their small paper packages through and which we sealed with wood putty after we moved in. That beautiful red metal table I found uptown somewhere and wrote my grant applications on before I left for Berlin. And the small carved box with the inlaid stones I left behind on the windowsill for the little Turkish girl who suddenly appeared through the hedge a few days before we left Fidicinstrasse, wanting to know a thousand things, what our names were, why we didn't have any children, our departure angel, but that came later, much later. I look around me and imagine that I have the wild look of a person who has five minutes to pack her things and flee, confused by this world of objects and all these fingerprints, all these footprints, and wonder how much of the present moment I will forget, and what new locations I pass by now and again without giving them a second thought, locations which will contain some new part of me, which will become irrevocably interwoven with this life, these objects I've collected, this body.